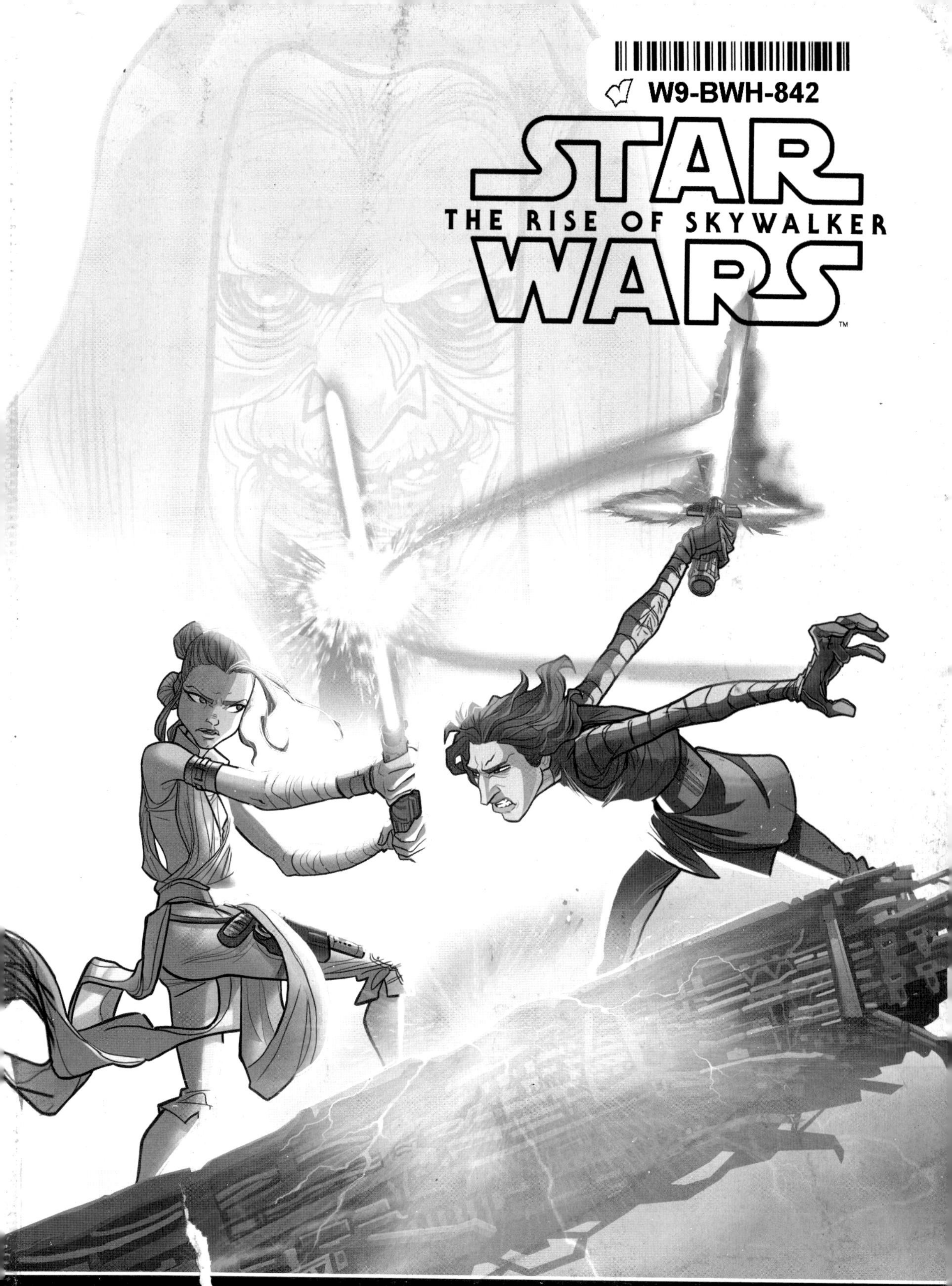
STAR WARS
THE RISE OF SKYWALKER

A LONG TIME AGO, IN A GALAXY FAR, FAR AWAY....

The End of
A JOURNEY

REY

There's something Rey has always wanted to know, ever since she was a scavenger on the remote planet of Jakku, living alone, removing valuable parts from the Imperial spacecraft abandoned there and selling them for food. **Who is she?**

When Rey was just a child, her parents left her on Jakku without ever returning, and she had to learn how to take care of herself. Years later, she saved a little astromech droid, BB-8, from another scavenger. Helping BB-8, Rey began an incredible journey that took her a long way from Jakku: she met General Leia Organa and joined the Resistance; she fought on Starkiller Base against the First Order and Kylo Ren, the son Leia and Han Solo lost to the dark side of the Force; and she started her training under legendary Jedi Master Luke Skywalker to learn the ways of the Force. Through it all she felt **a growing, enigmatic connection with Ren,** something neither of them could explain.

Now Rey is continuing her training, encouraged and guided by General Leia. But that question remains unanswered, and obscure visions haunt her days: terrifying whispers and prophecies, the throne of the Sith, the triumph of the dark side, and **herself as the new Dark Lord. Is this inevitable?** Is this the answer she is looking for? The only way to find out is to reach the shadowy world of Exegol, in the Unknown Regions, where Rey's destiny will finally be revealed.

KYLO REN

Once the most promising apprentice of Luke Skywalker, Ben Solo couldn't control the darkness rising inside him. Soon he let Snoke, the Supreme Leader of the First Order, seduce him to the dark side of the Force. **He chose a path of no return.**

Feeling betrayed by his former master, Ben destroyed the Jedi Temple Skywalker built and became Kylo Ren. Under Snoke's guidance, Ren became stronger and angrier. To prove his commitment to the dark side, **he killed his father,** Han Solo, on Starkiller Base. It should have been the final act of his training, but that horrible event changed him in a way he couldn't expect. Moreover, the duel with an unknown scavenger from Jakku, who was able to defeat him, undermined his already torn mind. **The Force pushed Ben and Rey together** and made them share a unique bond: Kylo Ren therefore realized he could defeat Snoke and rule the galaxy with her. But after he killed his second master, Ren couldn't persuade Rey to join him. Left alone, he became the new Supreme Leader of the First Order and started to rampage from world to world, crushing any resistance movement, strengthening his authority. **And yet, someone is threatening his power:** a mysterious figure who was above Snoke, a powerful entity hiding in the shadows of Exegol. Finding him will be hard, killing him may be impossible…

Enemies and FRIENDS

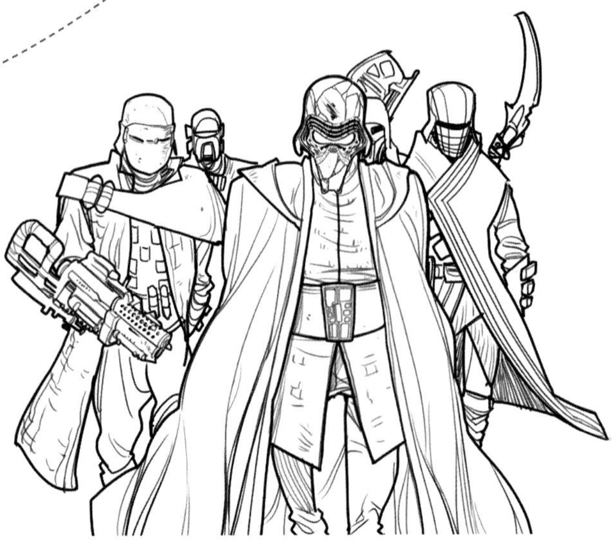

KNIGHTS OF REN

These Force-sensitive dark warriors are **Kylo Ren's personal sentinels.** Equipped with technologically modified primitive weapons and customized blasters, they are trained to face any opponent and capture any kind of prey. Their loyalty is based on fierceness: they'd never follow someone who could not prove to be the most powerful and ruthless in the galaxy.

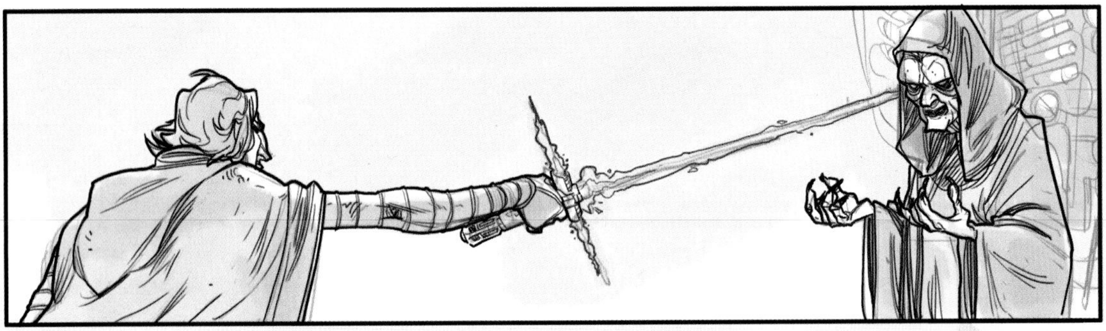

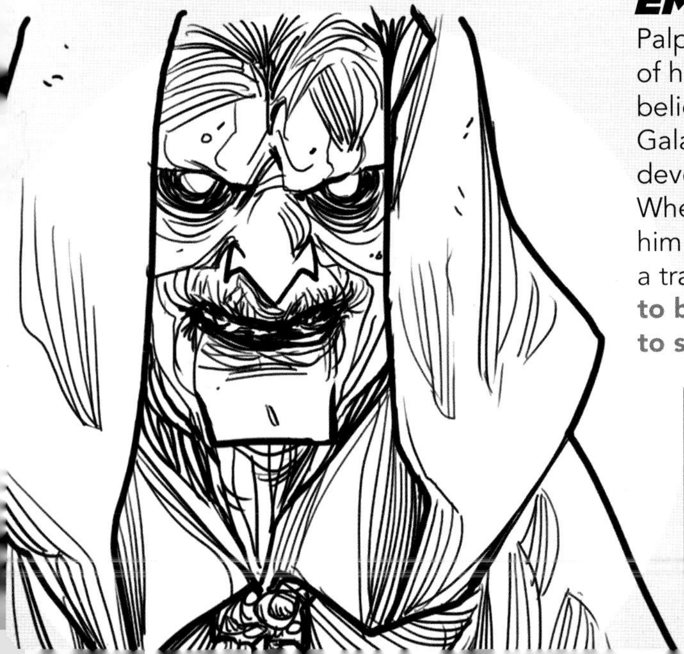

EMPEROR PALPATINE

Palpatine has always been a step ahead of his adversaries. While the Jedi Knights believed him to be just a Senator of the Galactic Republic, he was a Sith Lord devoted to the dark side of the Force. When the Rebels thought they could take him by surprise, he was luring them into a trap. **Now that everyone believes him to be dead, Palpatine reveals himself to still be alive.**

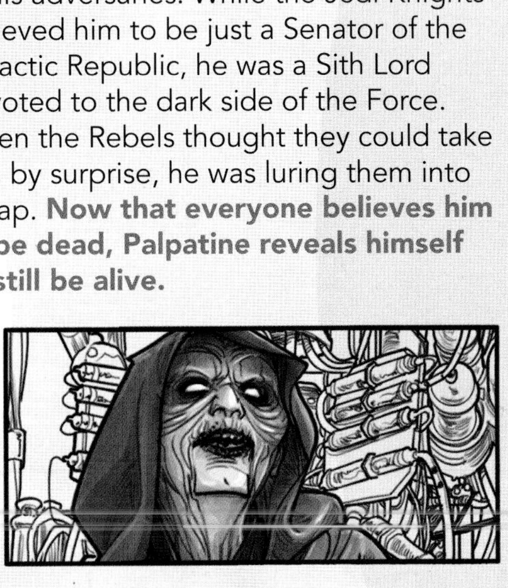

LUKE SKYWALKER

Projecting himself on Crait through the Force, deceiving Kylo Ren, and dragging him into a duel his former pupil could not win, Luke Skywalker **sacrificed himself to save Leia, the Resistance, and Rey.** But like other Jedi masters before him, Skywalker can now interact with the living as a Force ghost.

LANDO CALRISSIAN

A gambler who won an entire city in a card game. A war hero who helped destroy the second Death Star. This is Lando Calrissian, who **lost everything right when he was living a peaceful life.** After the fall of the Empire, in fact, his daughter was kidnapped by the First Order. Despite desperately searching for her, Lando could never find her.

THE RESISTANCE

For a year, after the Battle of Crait, **General Leia Organa recruited allies, trying to rebuild the Resistance** and face the forces of the First Order. Now that a new threat rises from the Unknown Regions, announcing the coming of an unbeatable fleet, Leia, together with Finn and Poe, could find herself in front of an impossible task.

Episode IX
THE RISE OF
SKYWALKER

The   dead   speak!
The galaxy has heard
a mysterious broadcast,
a threat of REVENGE in the
sinister voice of the late
EMPEROR PALPATINE.

GENERAL LEIA ORGANA
dispatches secret agents
to   gather   intelligence,
while REY, the last hope of the
Jedi, trains for battle against
the diabolical FIRST ORDER.

Meanwhile, Supreme Leader
KYLO REN rages in search of the
phantom Emperor, determined to
destroy any threat to his power....

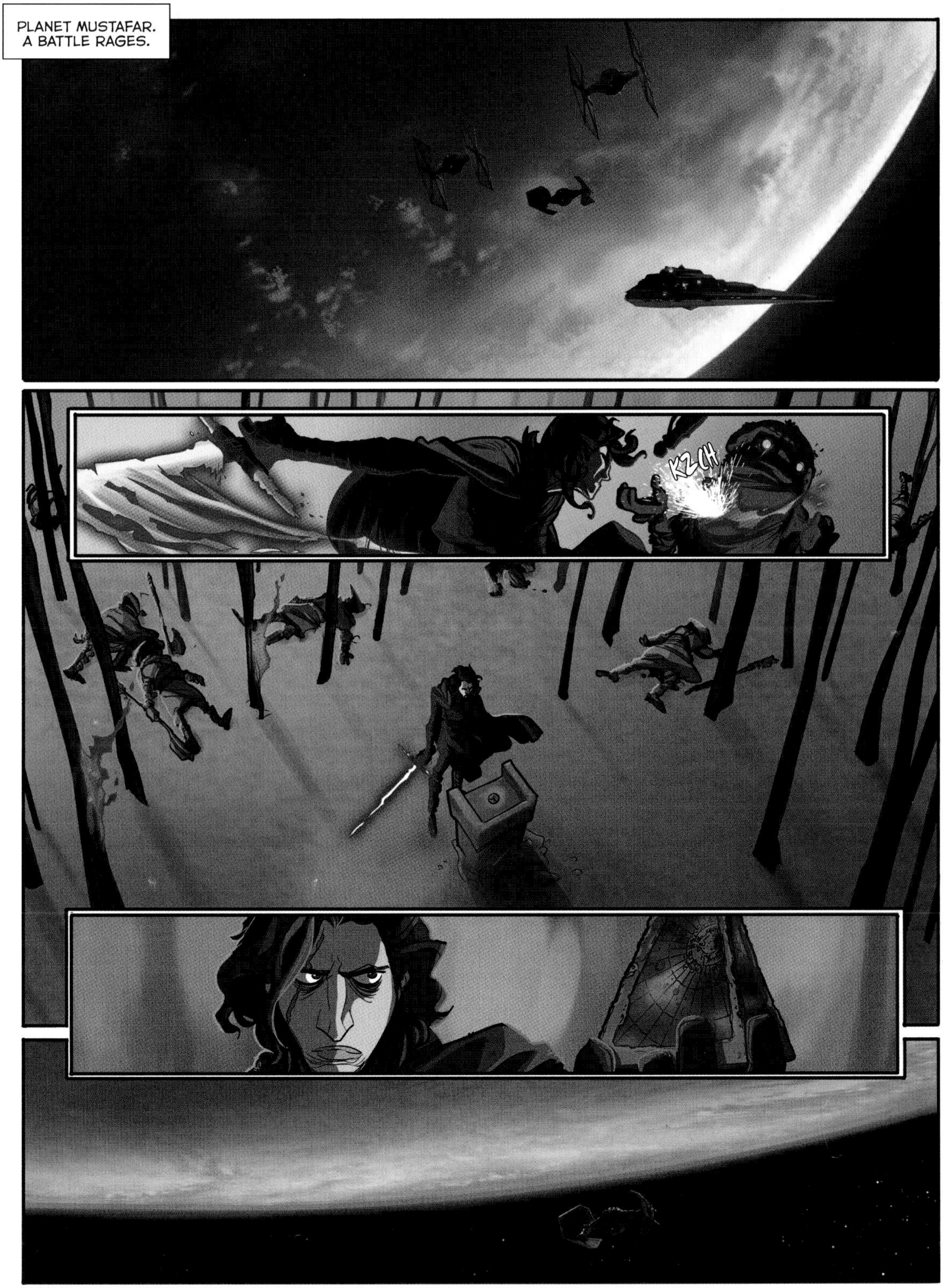

PLANET MUSTAFAR.
A BATTLE RAGES.
KZCH

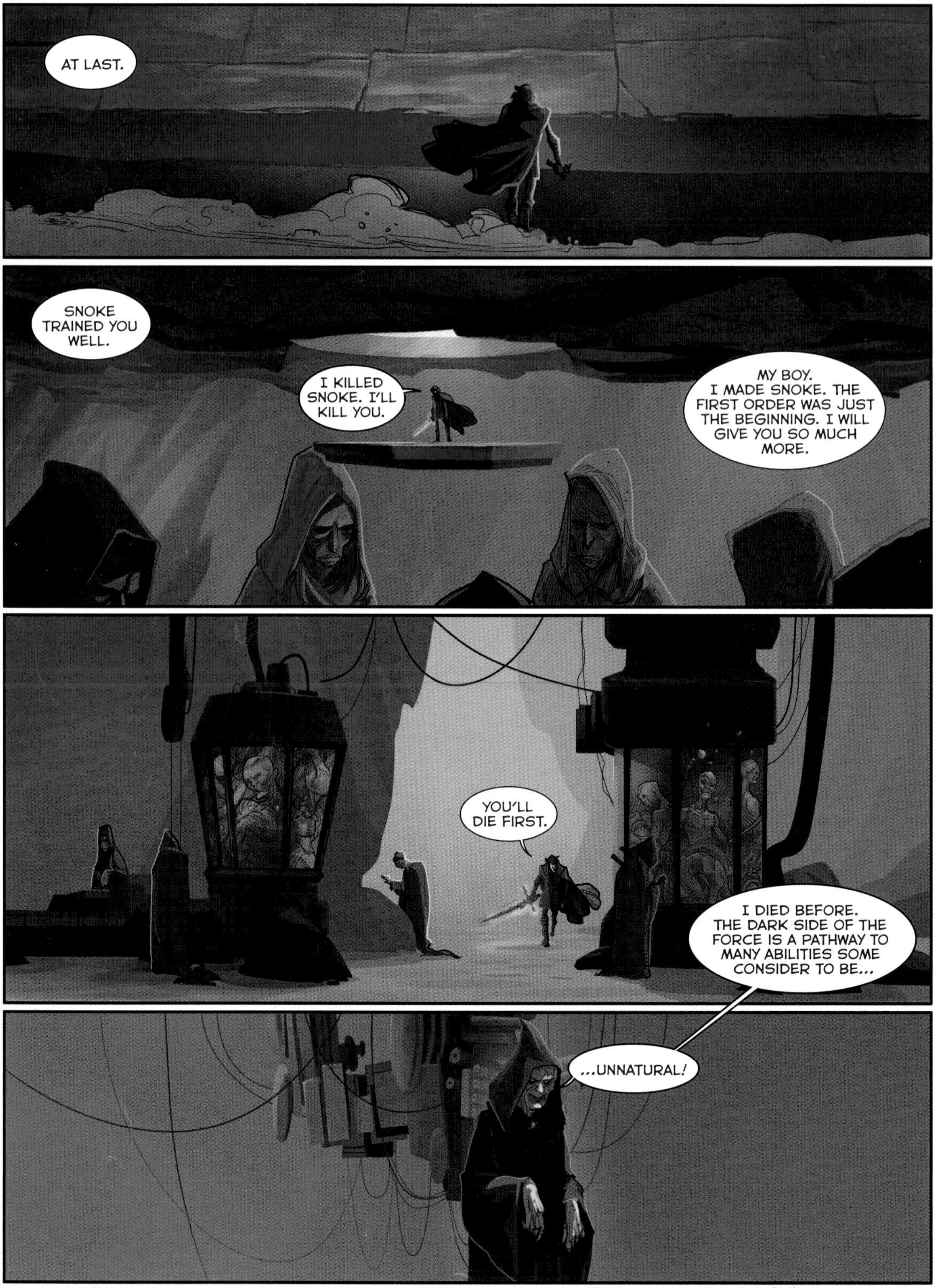
AT LAST.
SNOKE TRAINED YOU WELL.
I KILLED SNOKE. I'LL KILL YOU.
MY BOY. I MADE SNOKE. THE FIRST ORDER WAS JUST THE BEGINNING. I WILL GIVE YOU SO MUCH MORE.
YOU'LL DIE FIRST.
I DIED BEFORE. THE DARK SIDE OF THE FORCE IS A PATHWAY TO MANY ABILITIES SOME CONSIDER TO BE...
...UNNATURAL!

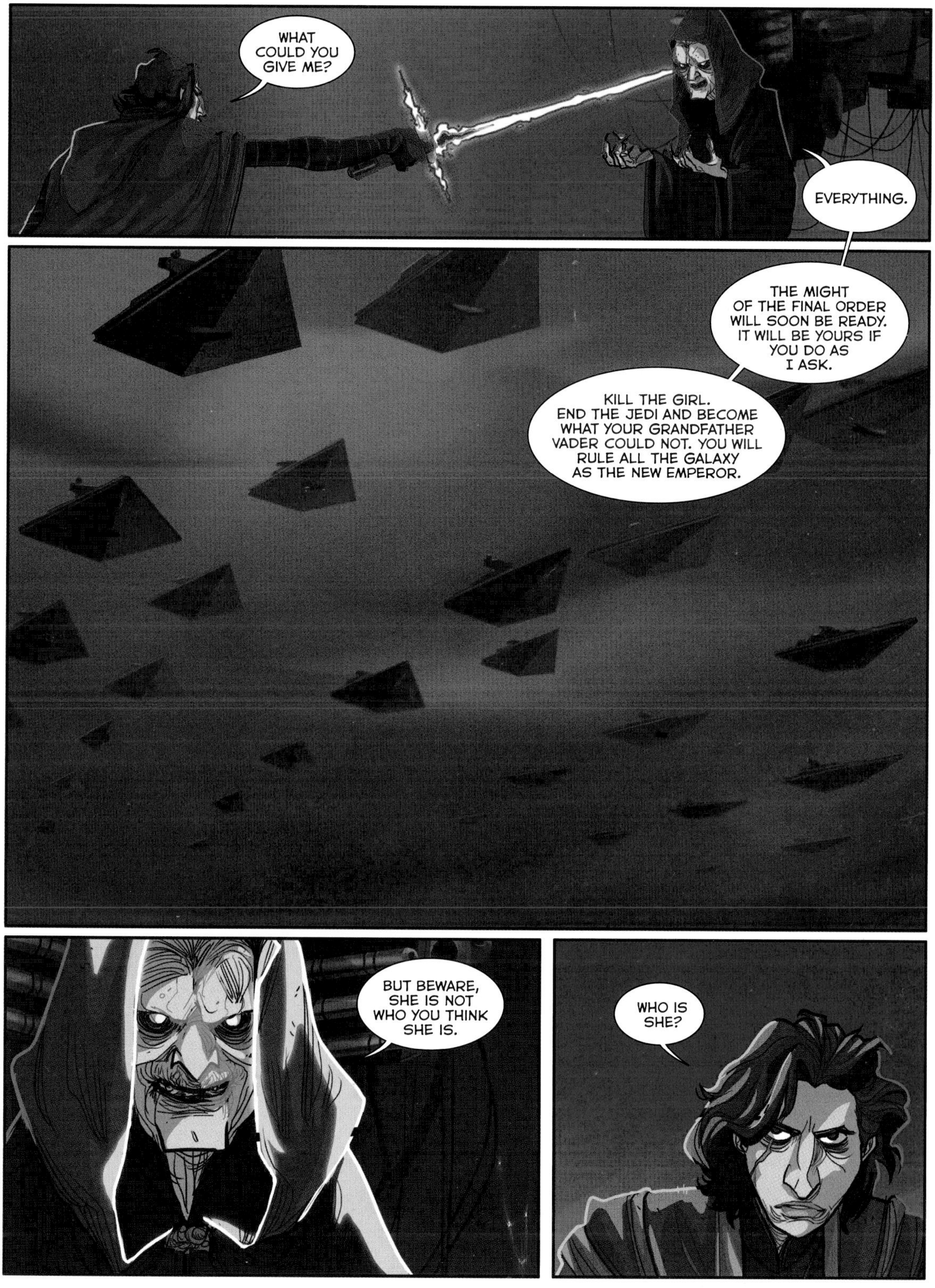
WHAT COULD YOU GIVE ME?
EVERYTHING.
THE MIGHT OF THE FINAL ORDER WILL SOON BE READY. IT WILL BE YOURS IF YOU DO AS I ASK.
KILL THE GIRL. END THE JEDI AND BECOME WHAT YOUR GRANDFATHER VADER COULD NOT. YOU WILL RULE ALL THE GALAXY AS THE NEW EMPEROR.
BUT BEWARE, SHE IS NOT WHO YOU THINK SHE IS.
WHO IS SHE?

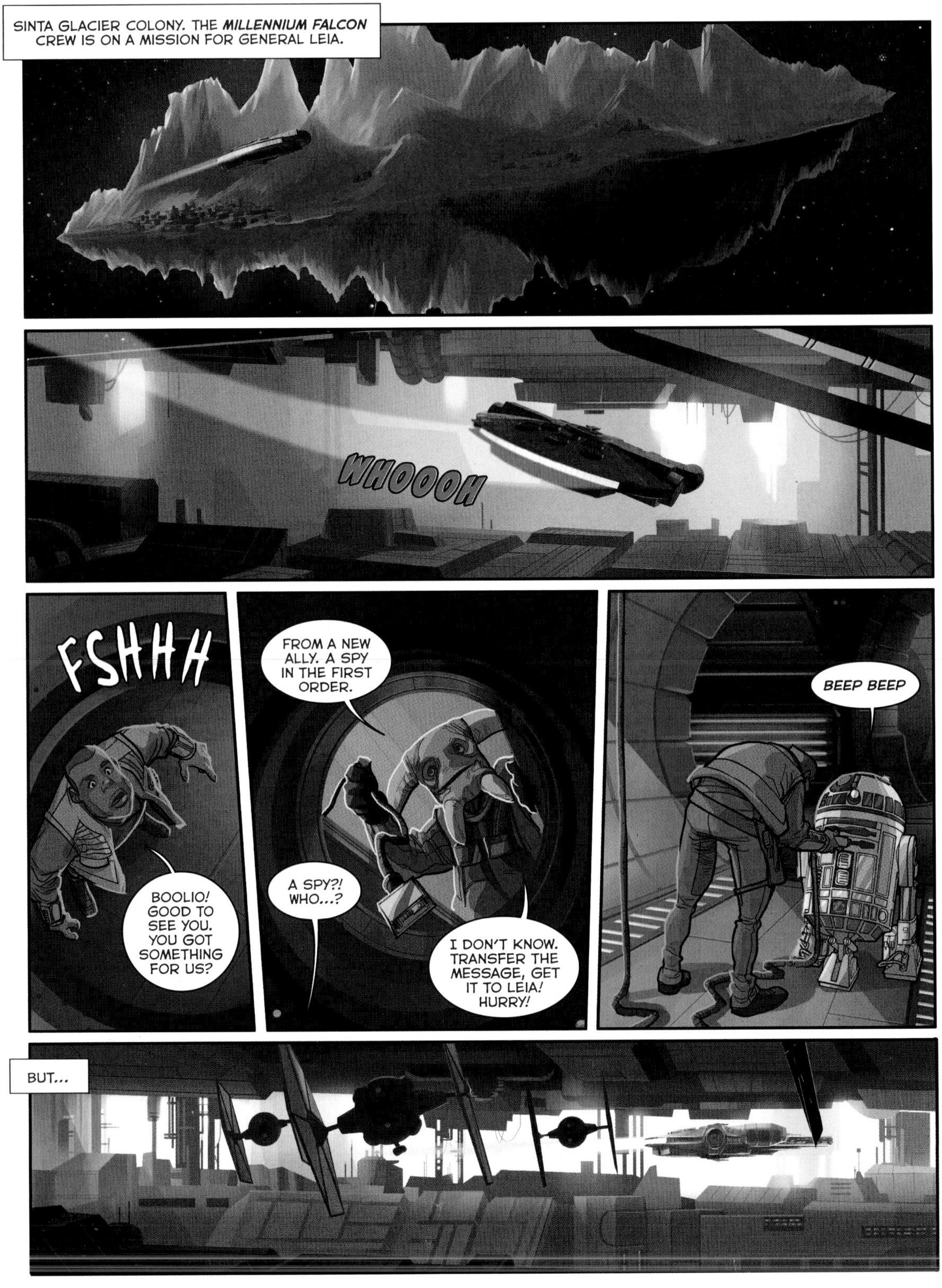
SINTA GLACIER COLONY. THE *MILLENNIUM FALCON* CREW IS ON A MISSION FOR GENERAL LEIA.
WHOOOH
FSHHH
BOOLIO! GOOD TO SEE YOU. YOU GOT SOMETHING FOR US?
FROM A NEW ALLY. A SPY IN THE FIRST ORDER.
A SPY?! WHO...?
I DON'T KNOW. TRANSFER THE MESSAGE, GET IT TO LEIA! HURRY!
BEEP BEEP
BUT...

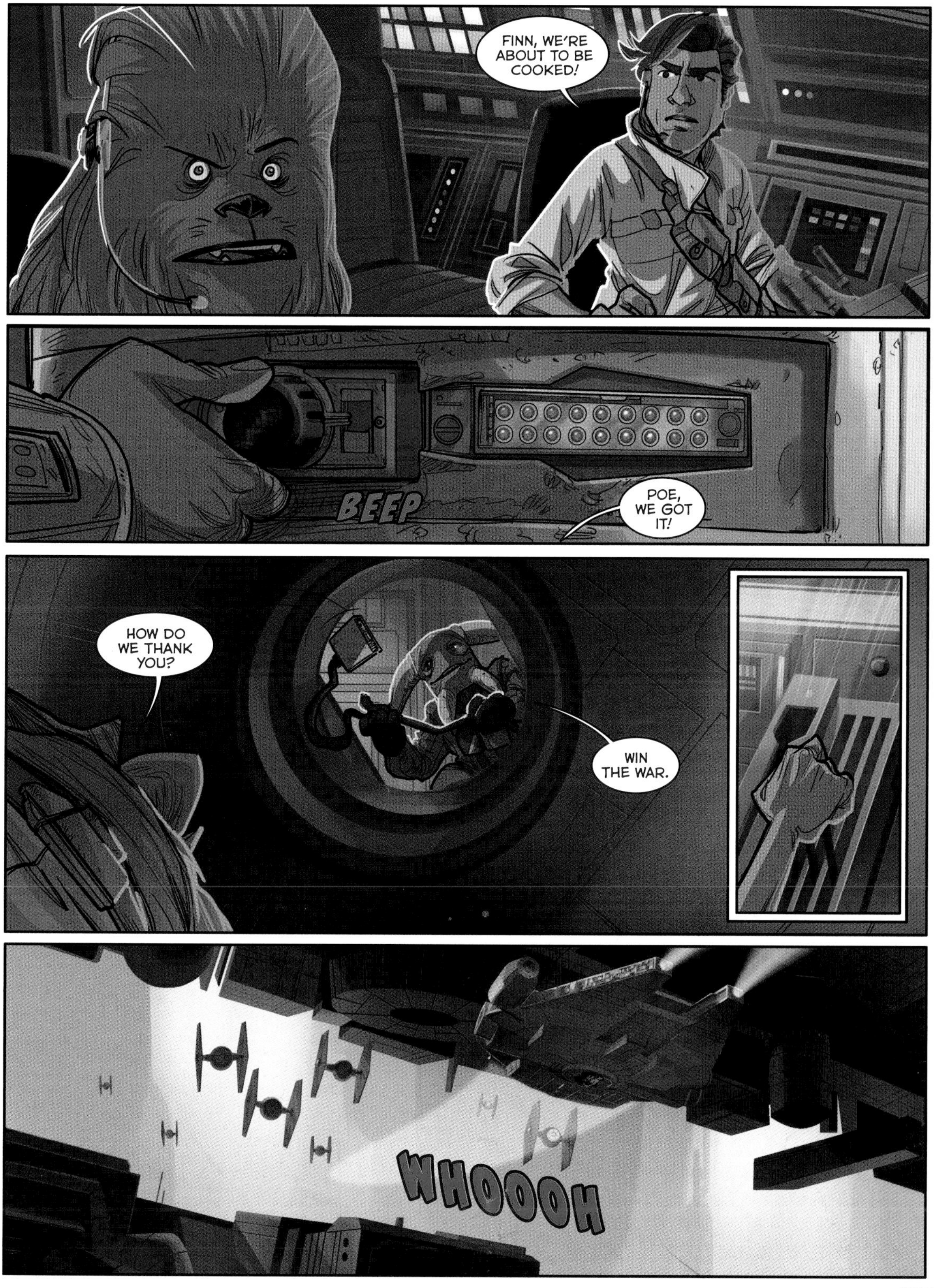
FINN, WE'RE ABOUT TO BE COOKED!
BEEP
POE, WE GOT IT!
HOW DO WE THANK YOU?
WIN THE WAR.
WHOOOH

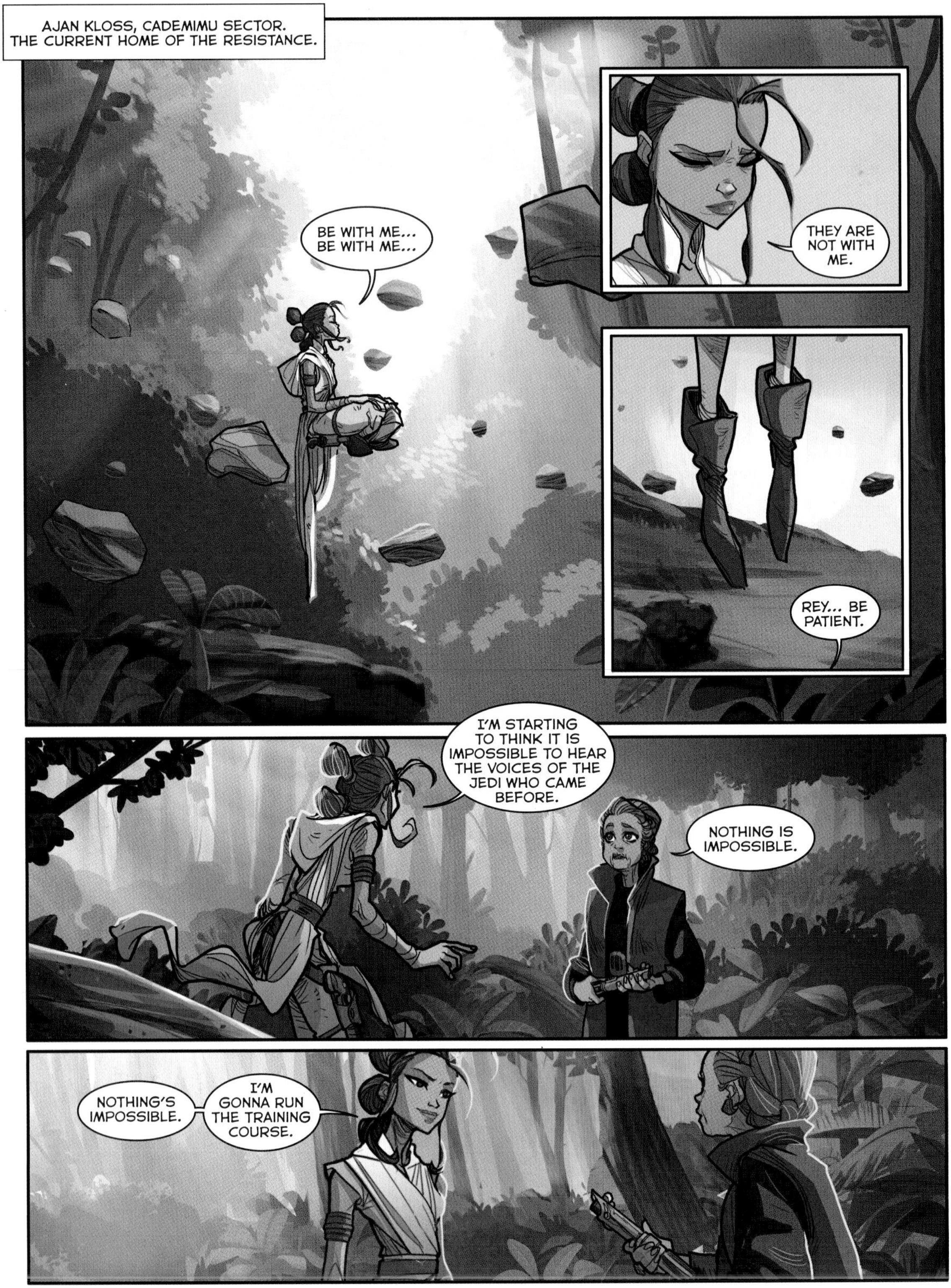

AJAN KLOSS, CADEMIMU SECTOR. THE CURRENT HOME OF THE RESISTANCE.
BE WITH ME... BE WITH ME...
THEY ARE NOT WITH ME.
REY... BE PATIENT.
I'M STARTING TO THINK IT IS IMPOSSIBLE TO HEAR THE VOICES OF THE JEDI WHO CAME BEFORE.
NOTHING IS IMPOSSIBLE.
NOTHING'S IMPOSSIBLE.
I'M GONNA RUN THE TRAINING COURSE.

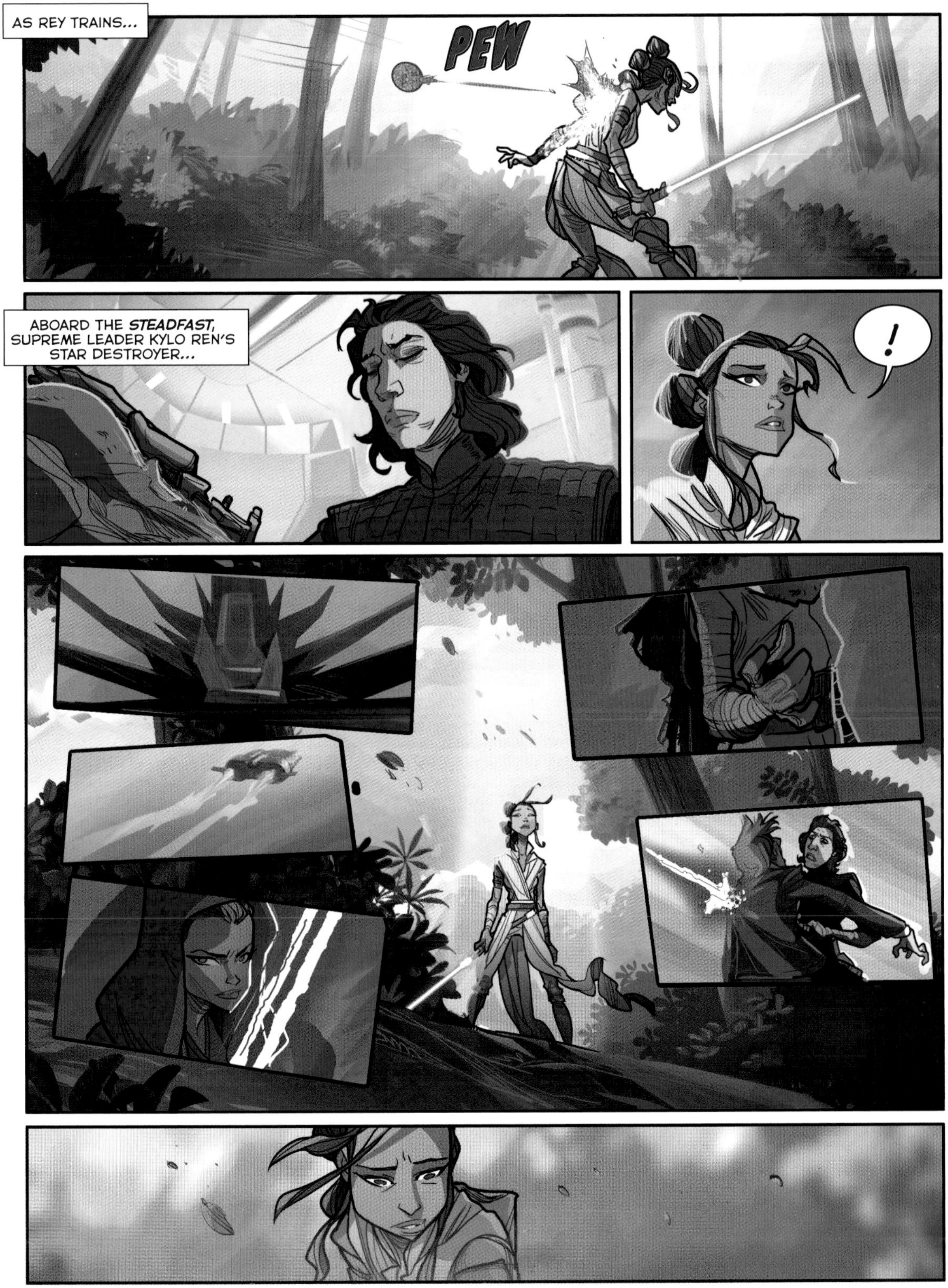
AS REY TRAINS...
PEW
ABOARD THE STEADFAST, SUPREME LEADER KYLO REN'S STAR DESTROYER...
!

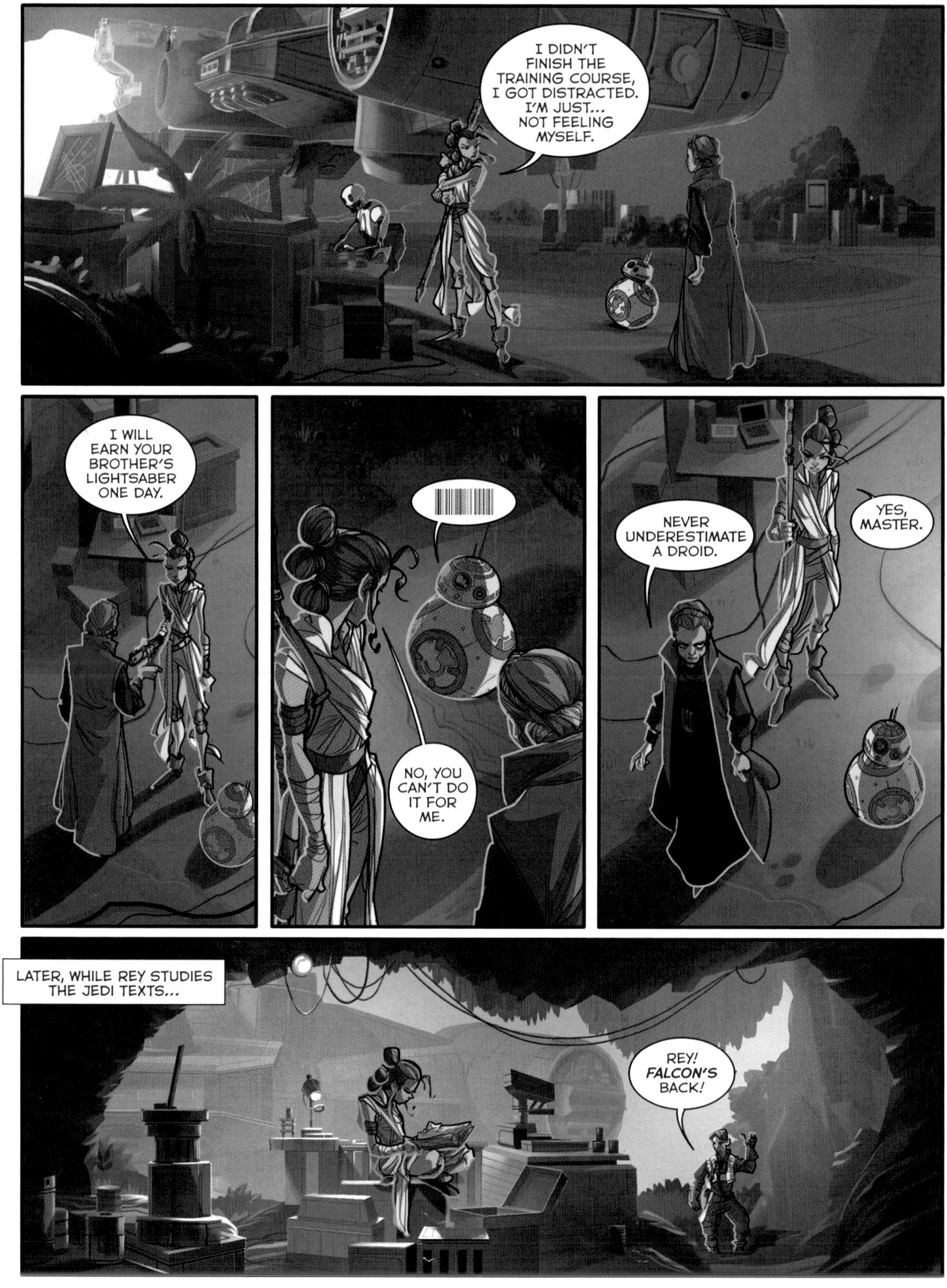
I DIDN'T FINISH THE TRAINING COURSE, I GOT DISTRACTED. I'M JUST... NOT FEELING MYSELF.
I WILL EARN YOUR BROTHER'S LIGHTSABER ONE DAY.
NO, YOU CAN'T DO IT FOR ME.
NEVER UNDERESTIMATE A DROID.
YES, MASTER.
LATER, WHILE REY STUDIES THE JEDI TEXTS...
REY! *FALCON'S* BACK!

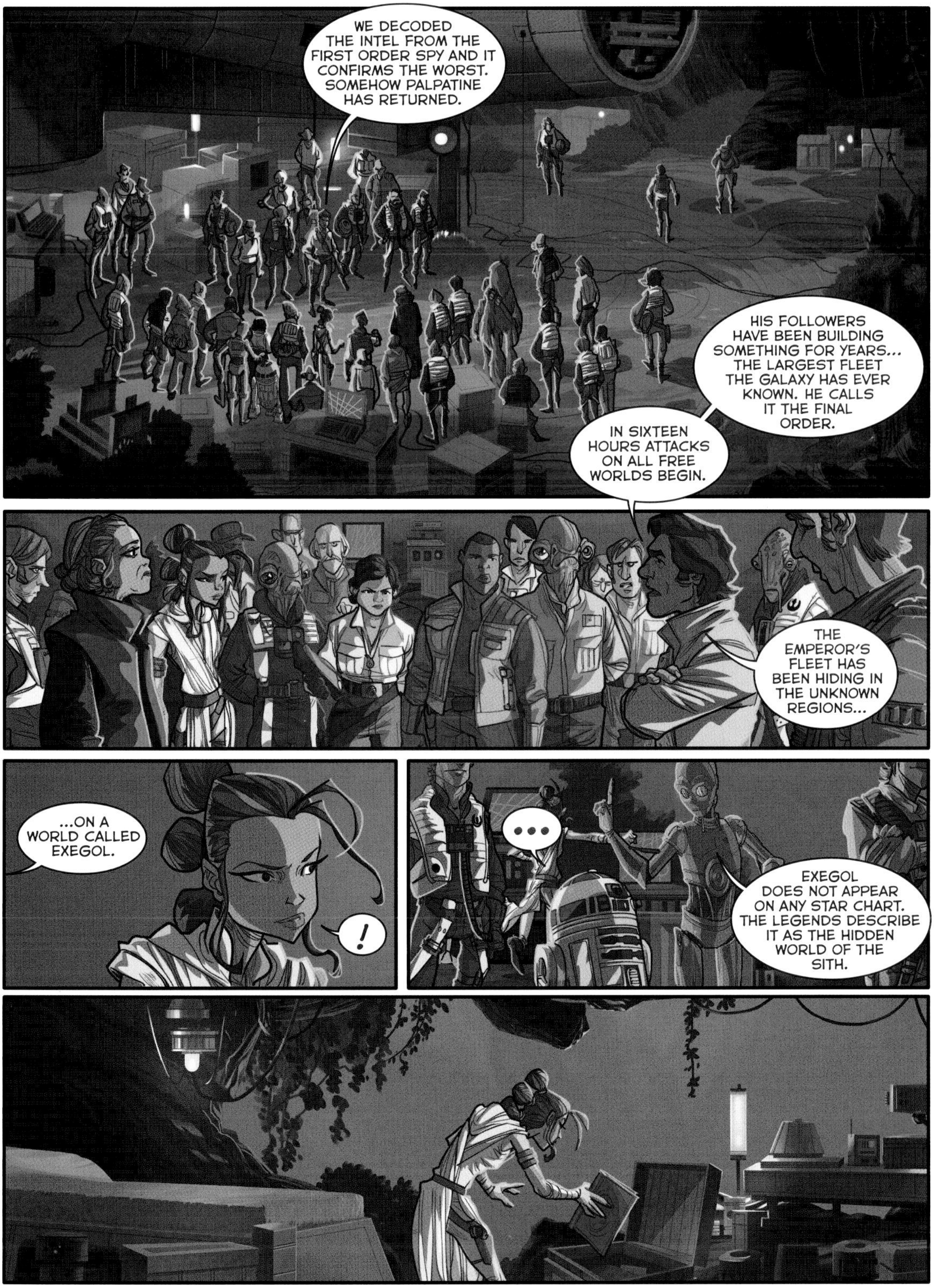

WE DECODED THE INTEL FROM THE FIRST ORDER SPY AND IT CONFIRMS THE WORST. SOMEHOW PALPATINE HAS RETURNED.
HIS FOLLOWERS HAVE BEEN BUILDING SOMETHING FOR YEARS... THE LARGEST FLEET THE GALAXY HAS EVER KNOWN. HE CALLS IT THE FINAL ORDER.
IN SIXTEEN HOURS ATTACKS ON ALL FREE WORLDS BEGIN.
THE EMPEROR'S FLEET HAS BEEN HIDING IN THE UNKNOWN REGIONS...
...ON A WORLD CALLED EXEGOL.
!
...
EXEGOL DOES NOT APPEAR ON ANY STAR CHART. THE LEGENDS DESCRIBE IT AS THE HIDDEN WORLD OF THE SITH.

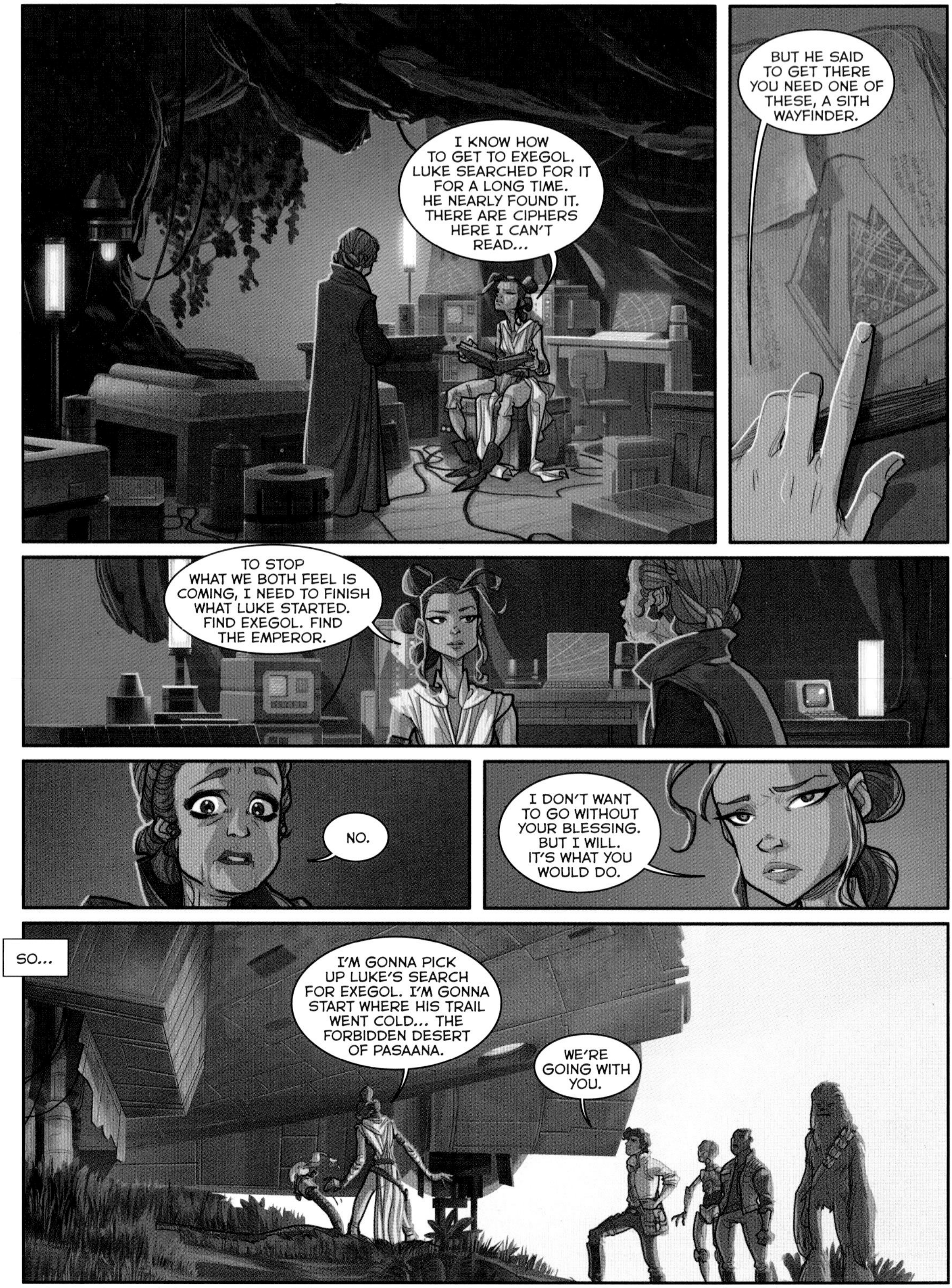
I KNOW HOW TO GET TO EXEGOL. LUKE SEARCHED FOR IT FOR A LONG TIME. HE NEARLY FOUND IT. THERE ARE CIPHERS HERE I CAN'T READ...
BUT HE SAID TO GET THERE YOU NEED ONE OF THESE, A SITH WAYFINDER.
TO STOP WHAT WE BOTH FEEL IS COMING, I NEED TO FINISH WHAT LUKE STARTED. FIND EXEGOL. FIND THE EMPEROR.
NO.
I DON'T WANT TO GO WITHOUT YOUR BLESSING. BUT I WILL. IT'S WHAT YOU WOULD DO.
SO...
I'M GONNA PICK UP LUKE'S SEARCH FOR EXEGOL. I'M GONNA START WHERE HIS TRAIL WENT COLD... THE FORBIDDEN DESERT OF PASAANA.
WE'RE GOING WITH YOU.

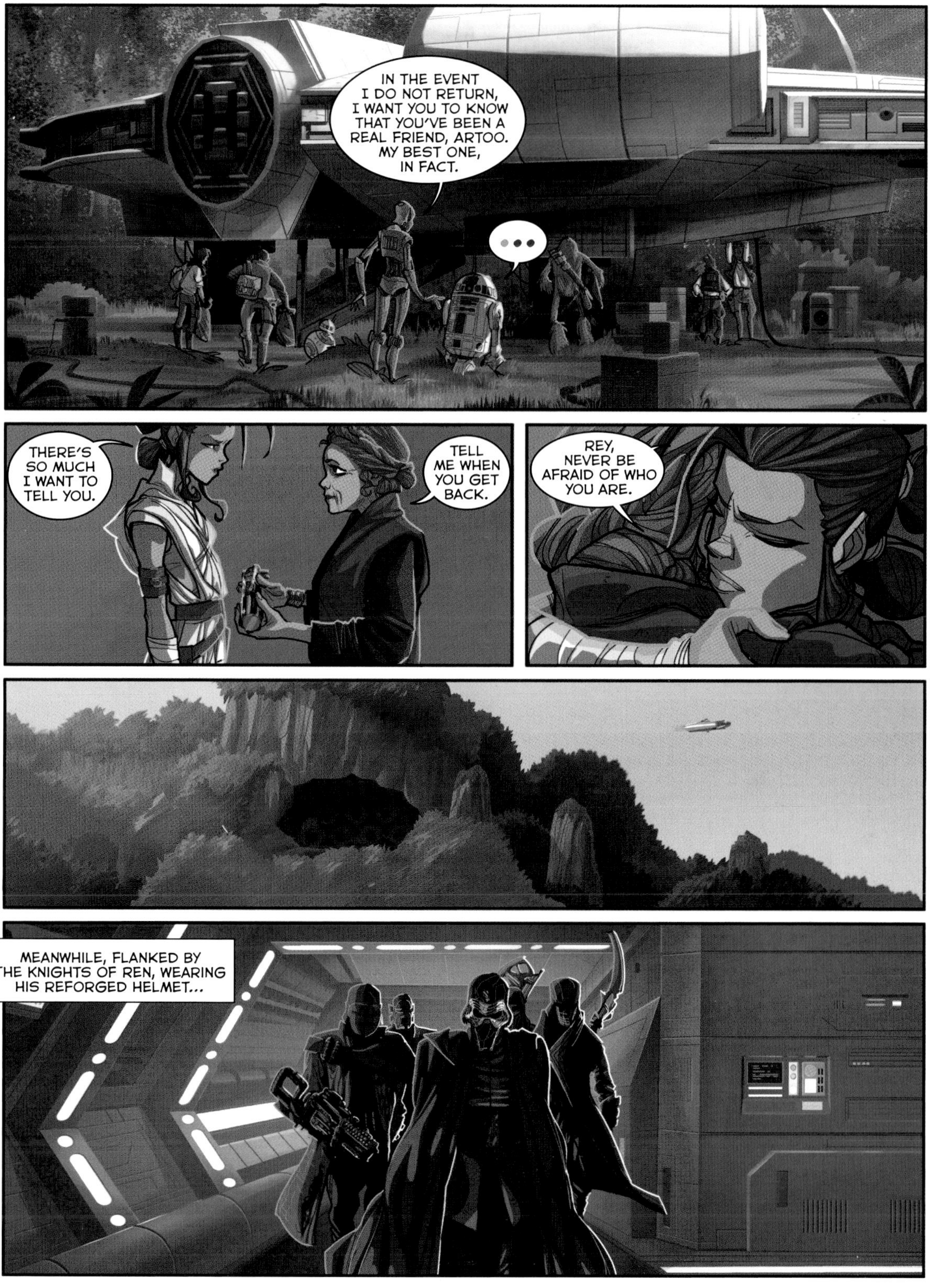

IN THE EVENT I DO NOT RETURN, I WANT YOU TO KNOW THAT YOU'VE BEEN A REAL FRIEND, ARTOO. MY BEST ONE, IN FACT.
...
THERE'S SO MUCH I WANT TO TELL YOU.
TELL ME WHEN YOU GET BACK.
REY, NEVER BE AFRAID OF WHO YOU ARE.
MEANWHILE, FLANKED BY THE KNIGHTS OF REN, WEARING HIS REFORGED HELMET...

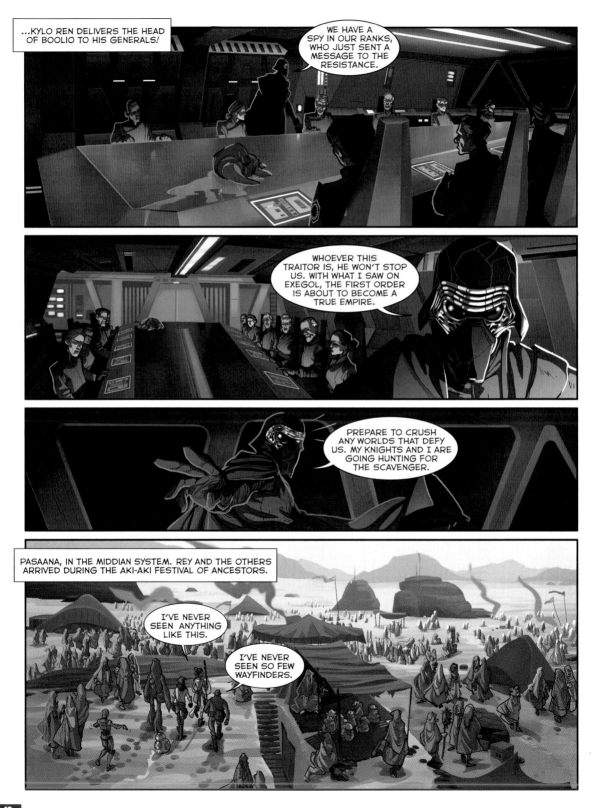

...KYLO REN DELIVERS THE HEAD OF BOOLIO TO HIS GENERALS!

WE HAVE A SPY IN OUR RANKS, WHO JUST SENT A MESSAGE TO THE RESISTANCE.

WHOEVER THIS TRAITOR IS, HE WON'T STOP US. WITH WHAT I SAW ON EXEGOL, THE FIRST ORDER IS ABOUT TO BECOME A TRUE EMPIRE.

PREPARE TO CRUSH ANY WORLDS THAT DEFY US. MY KNIGHTS AND I ARE GOING HUNTING FOR THE SCAVENGER.

PASAANA, IN THE MIDDIAN SYSTEM. REY AND THE OTHERS ARRIVED DURING THE AKI-AKI FESTIVAL OF ANCESTORS.

I'VE NEVER SEEN ANYTHING LIKE THIS.

I'VE NEVER SEEN SO FEW WAYFINDERS.

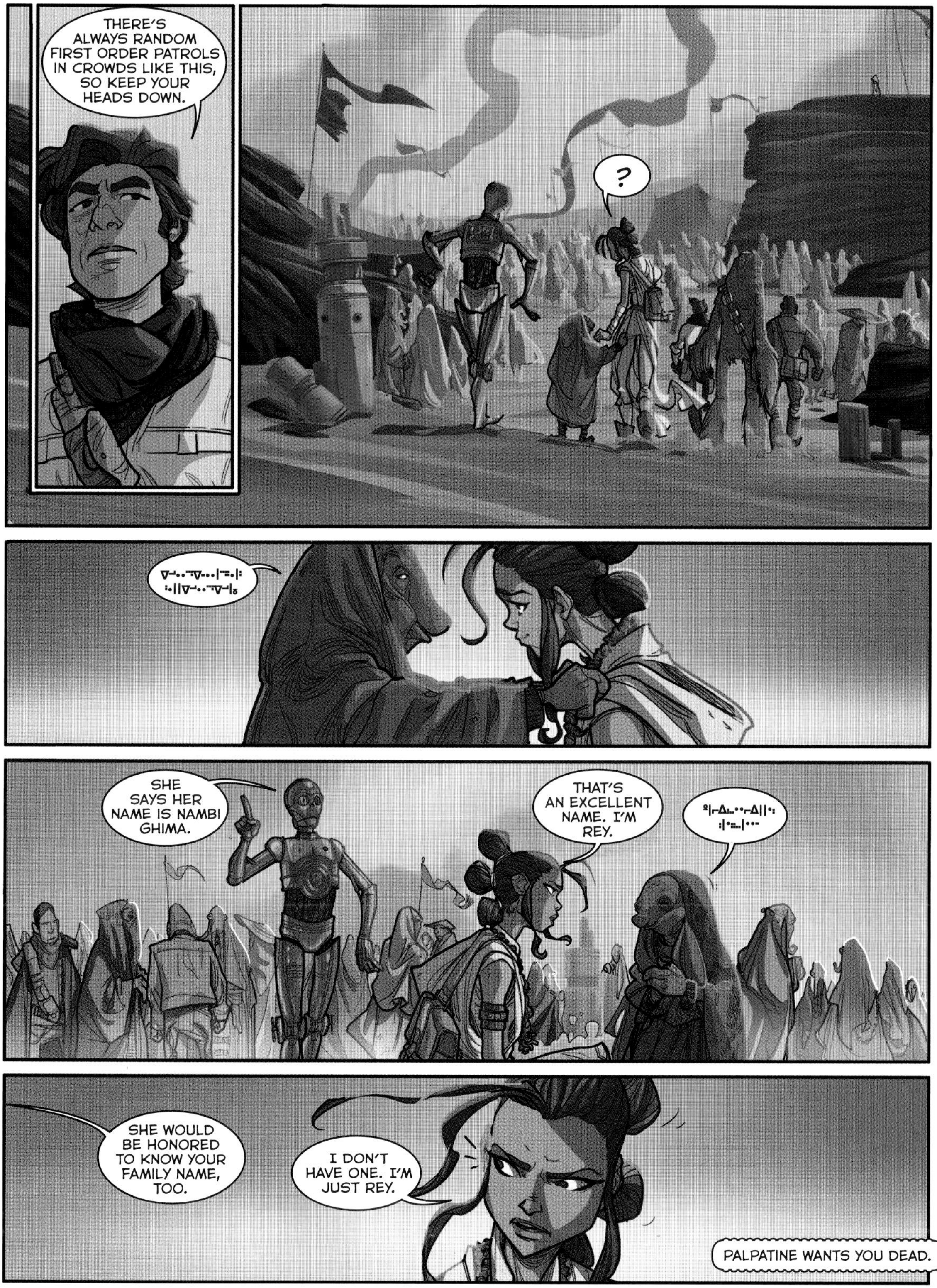
THERE'S ALWAYS RANDOM FIRST ORDER PATROLS IN CROWDS LIKE THIS, SO KEEP YOUR HEADS DOWN.
?
SHE SAYS HER NAME IS NAMBI GHIMA.
THAT'S AN EXCELLENT NAME. I'M REY.
SHE WOULD BE HONORED TO KNOW YOUR FAMILY NAME, TOO.
I DON'T HAVE ONE. I'M JUST REY.
PALPATINE WANTS YOU DEAD.

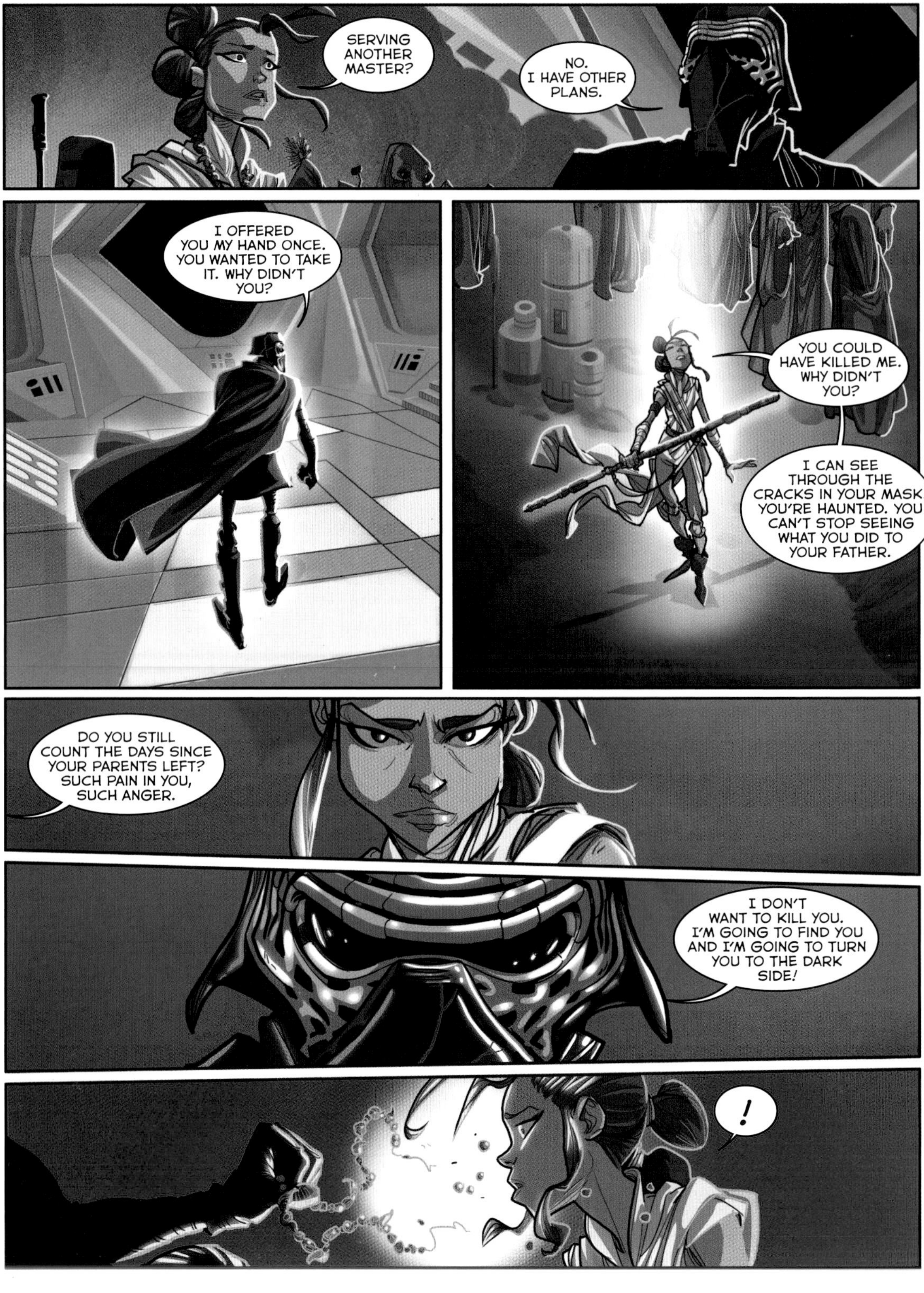
SERVING ANOTHER MASTER?
NO. I HAVE OTHER PLANS.
I OFFERED YOU MY HAND ONCE. YOU WANTED TO TAKE IT. WHY DIDN'T YOU?
YOU COULD HAVE KILLED ME. WHY DIDN'T YOU?
I CAN SEE THROUGH THE CRACKS IN YOUR MASK. YOU'RE HAUNTED. YOU CAN'T STOP SEEING WHAT YOU DID TO YOUR FATHER.
DO YOU STILL COUNT THE DAYS SINCE YOUR PARENTS LEFT? SUCH PAIN IN YOU, SUCH ANGER.
I DON'T WANT TO KILL YOU. I'M GOING TO FIND YOU AND I'M GOING TO TURN YOU TO THE DARK SIDE!
!

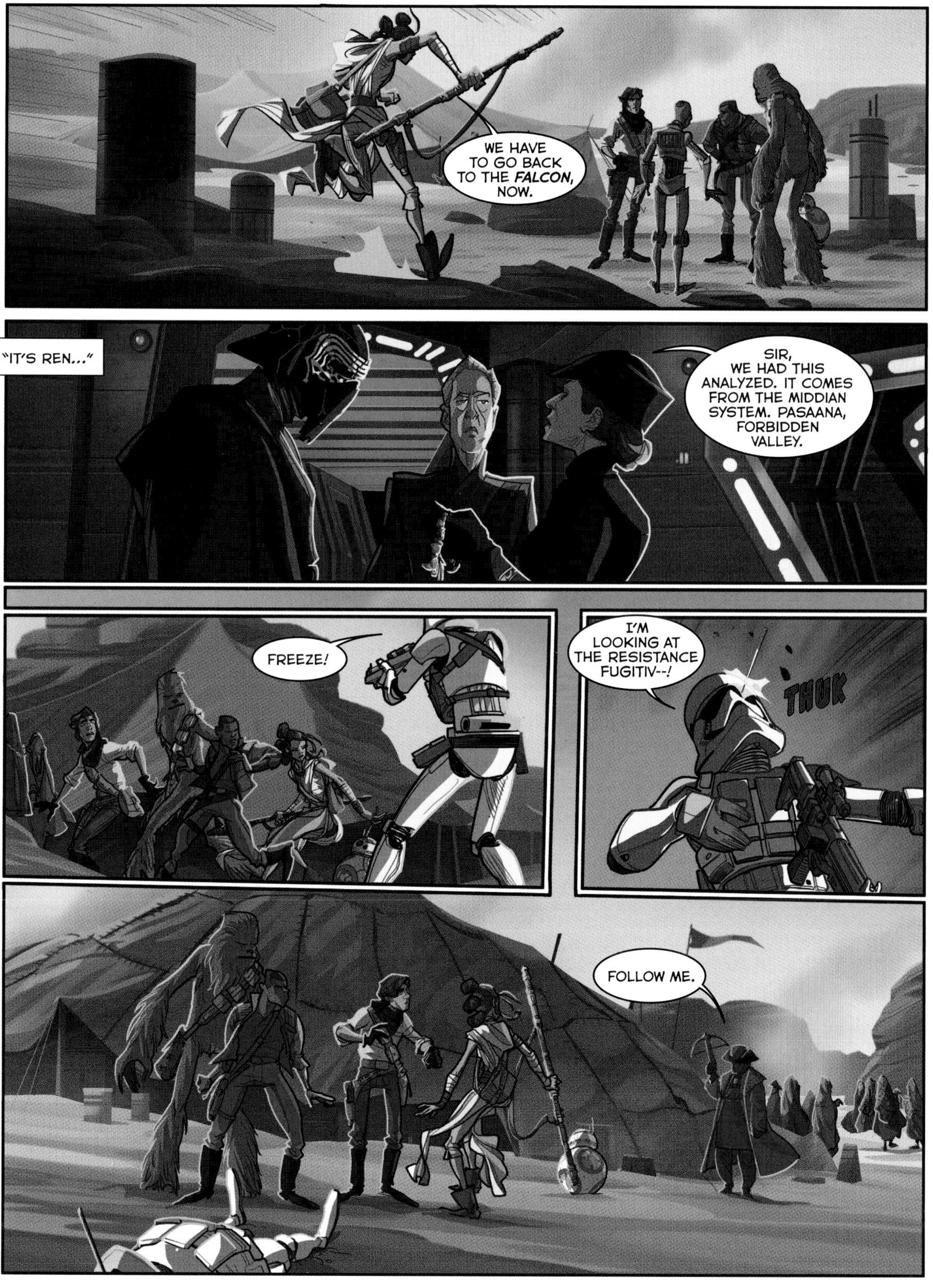
WE HAVE TO GO BACK TO THE *FALCON*, NOW.
"IT'S REN..."
SIR, WE HAD THIS ANALYZED. IT COMES FROM THE MIDDIAN SYSTEM. PASAANA, FORBIDDEN VALLEY.
FREEZE!
I'M LOOKING AT THE RESISTANCE FUGITIV--!
THUK
FOLLOW ME.

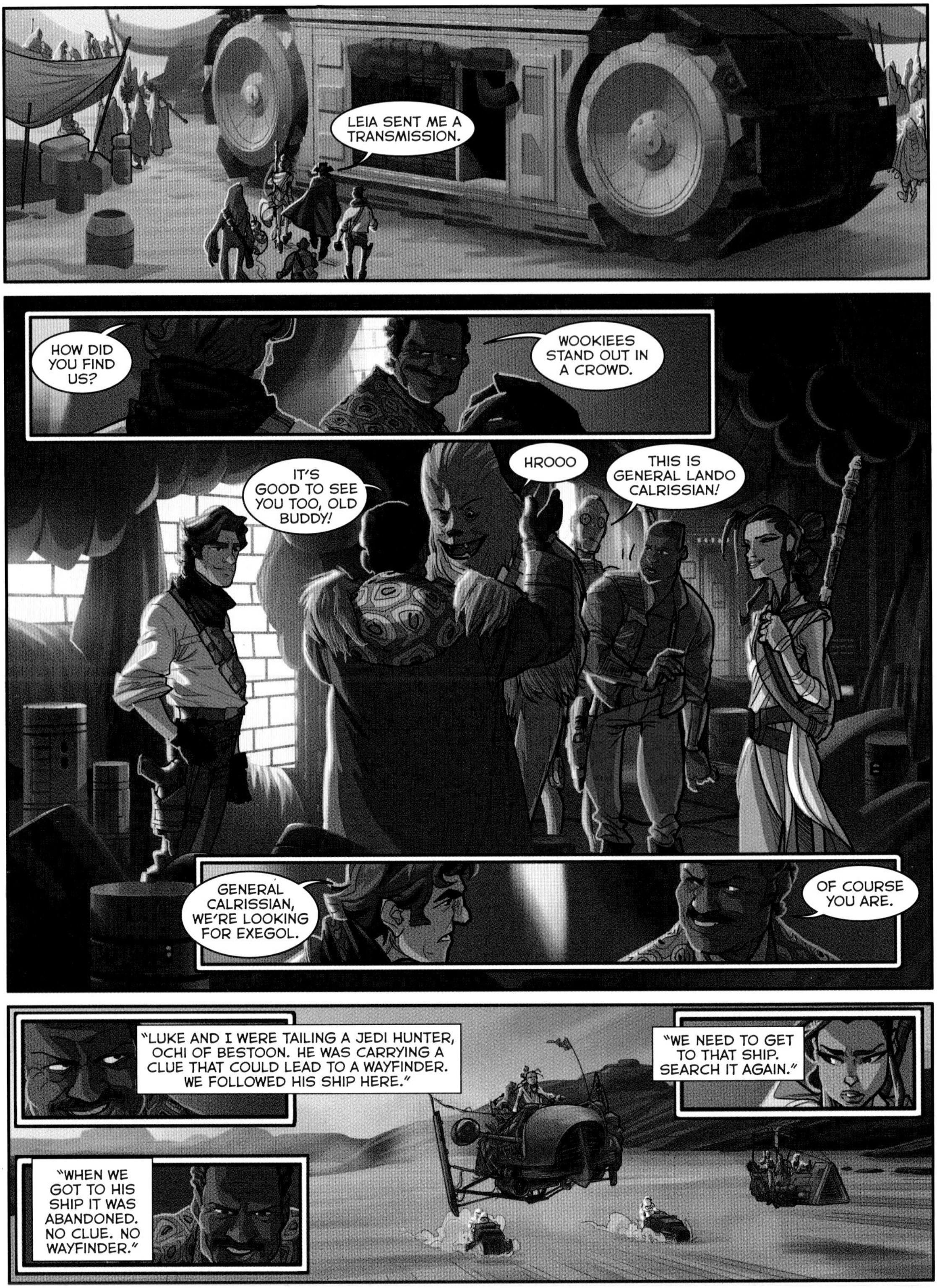
LEIA SENT ME A TRANSMISSION.
HOW DID YOU FIND US?
WOOKIEES STAND OUT IN A CROWD.
IT'S GOOD TO SEE YOU TOO, OLD BUDDY!
HROOO
THIS IS GENERAL LANDO CALRISSIAN!
GENERAL CALRISSIAN, WE'RE LOOKING FOR EXEGOL.
OF COURSE YOU ARE.
"LUKE AND I WERE TAILING A JEDI HUNTER, OCHI OF BESTOON. HE WAS CARRYING A CLUE THAT COULD LEAD TO A WAYFINDER. WE FOLLOWED HIS SHIP HERE."
"WHEN WE GOT TO HIS SHIP IT WAS ABANDONED. NO CLUE. NO WAYFINDER."
"WE NEED TO GET TO THAT SHIP. SEARCH IT AGAIN."

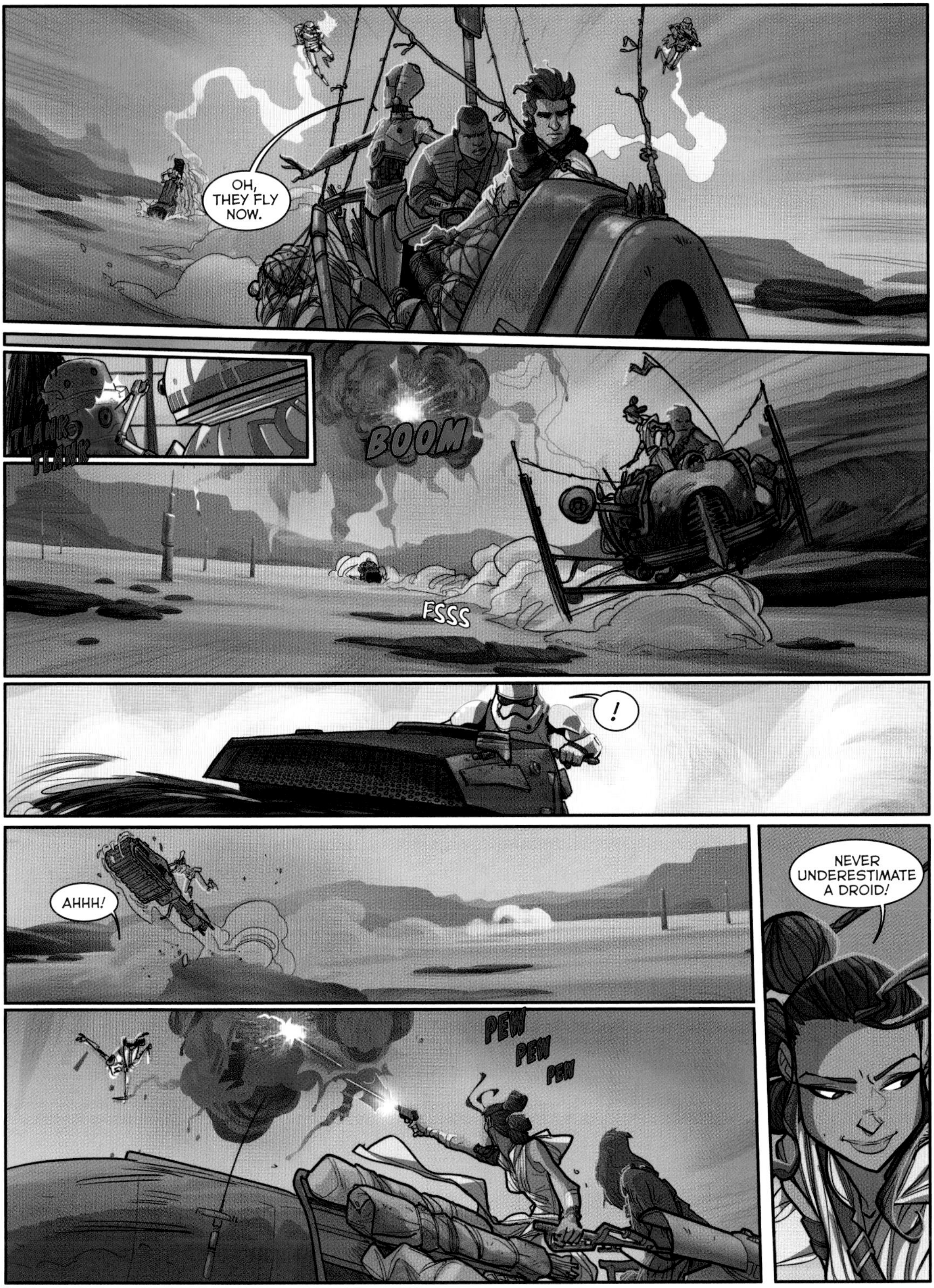
OH, THEY FLY NOW.
TLANK TLANK
BOOM
FSSS
!
AHHH!
NEVER UNDERESTIMATE A DROID!
PEW PEW PEW

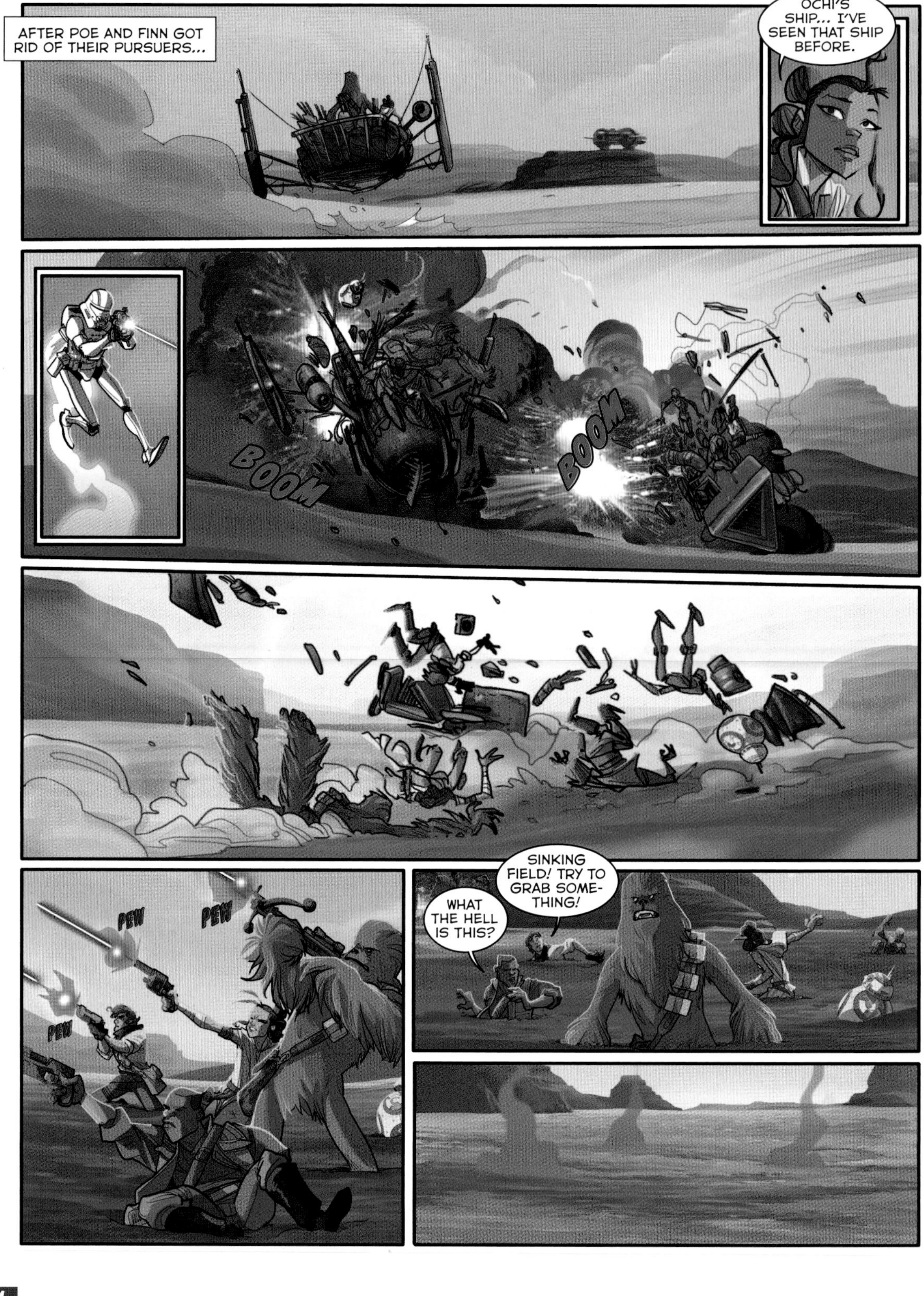
AFTER POE AND FINN GOT RID OF THEIR PURSUERS...
OCHI'S SHIP... I'VE SEEN THAT SHIP BEFORE.
BOOM
BOOM
PEW
PEW
PEW
SINKING FIELD! TRY TO GRAB SOME-THING!
WHAT THE HELL IS THIS?

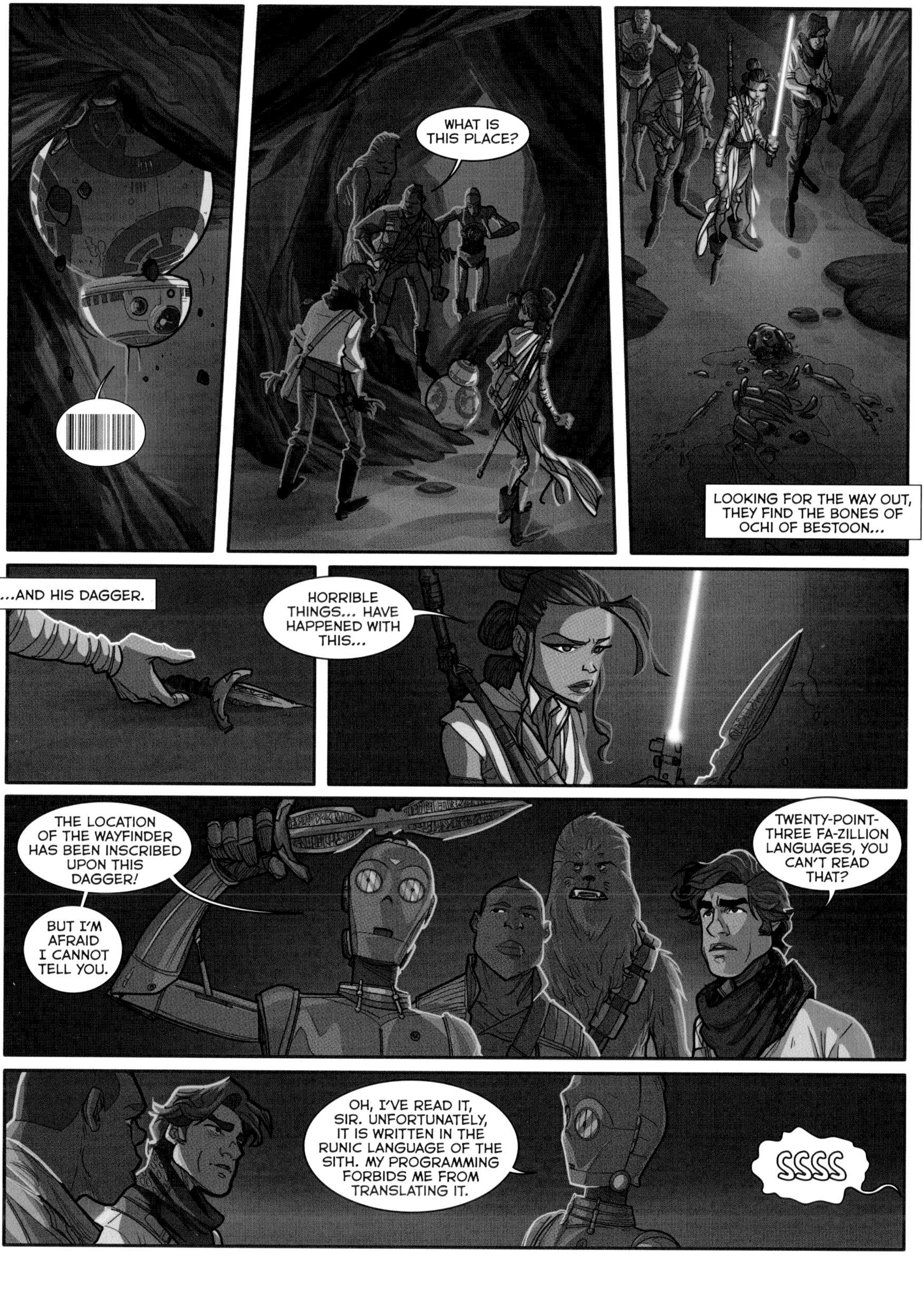
WHAT IS THIS PLACE?
LOOKING FOR THE WAY OUT, THEY FIND THE BONES OF OCHI OF BESTOON...
...AND HIS DAGGER.
HORRIBLE THINGS... HAVE HAPPENED WITH THIS...
THE LOCATION OF THE WAYFINDER HAS BEEN INSCRIBED UPON THIS DAGGER!
BUT I'M AFRAID I CANNOT TELL YOU.
TWENTY-POINT-THREE FA-ZILLION LANGUAGES, YOU CAN'T READ THAT?
OH, I'VE READ IT, SIR. UNFORTUNATELY, IT IS WRITTEN IN THE RUNIC LANGUAGE OF THE SITH. MY PROGRAMMING FORBIDS ME FROM TRANSLATING IT.
SSSS

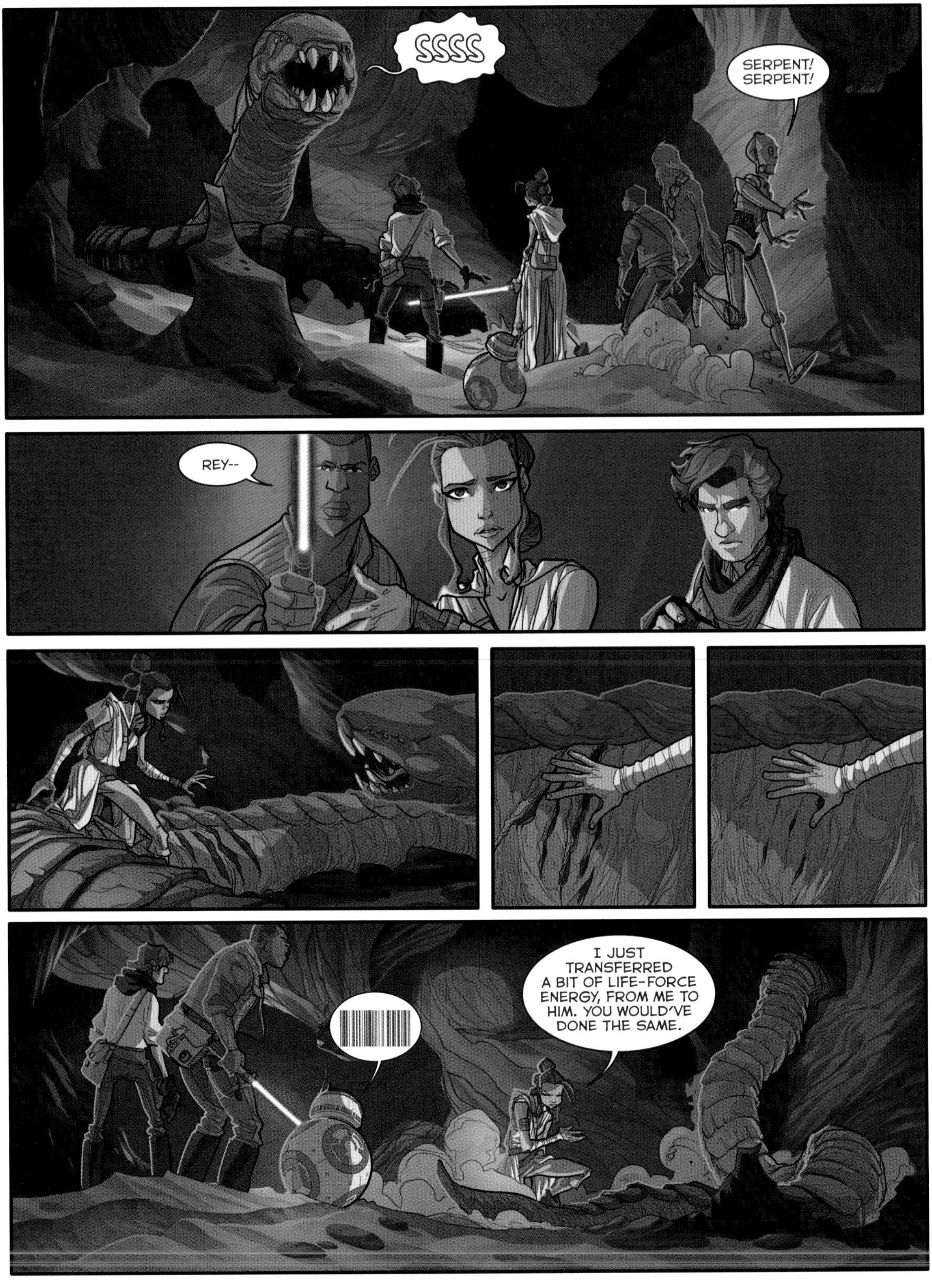
SSSS
SERPENT! SERPENT!
REY--
I JUST TRANSFERRED A BIT OF LIFE-FORCE ENERGY, FROM ME TO HIM. YOU WOULD'VE DONE THE SAME.

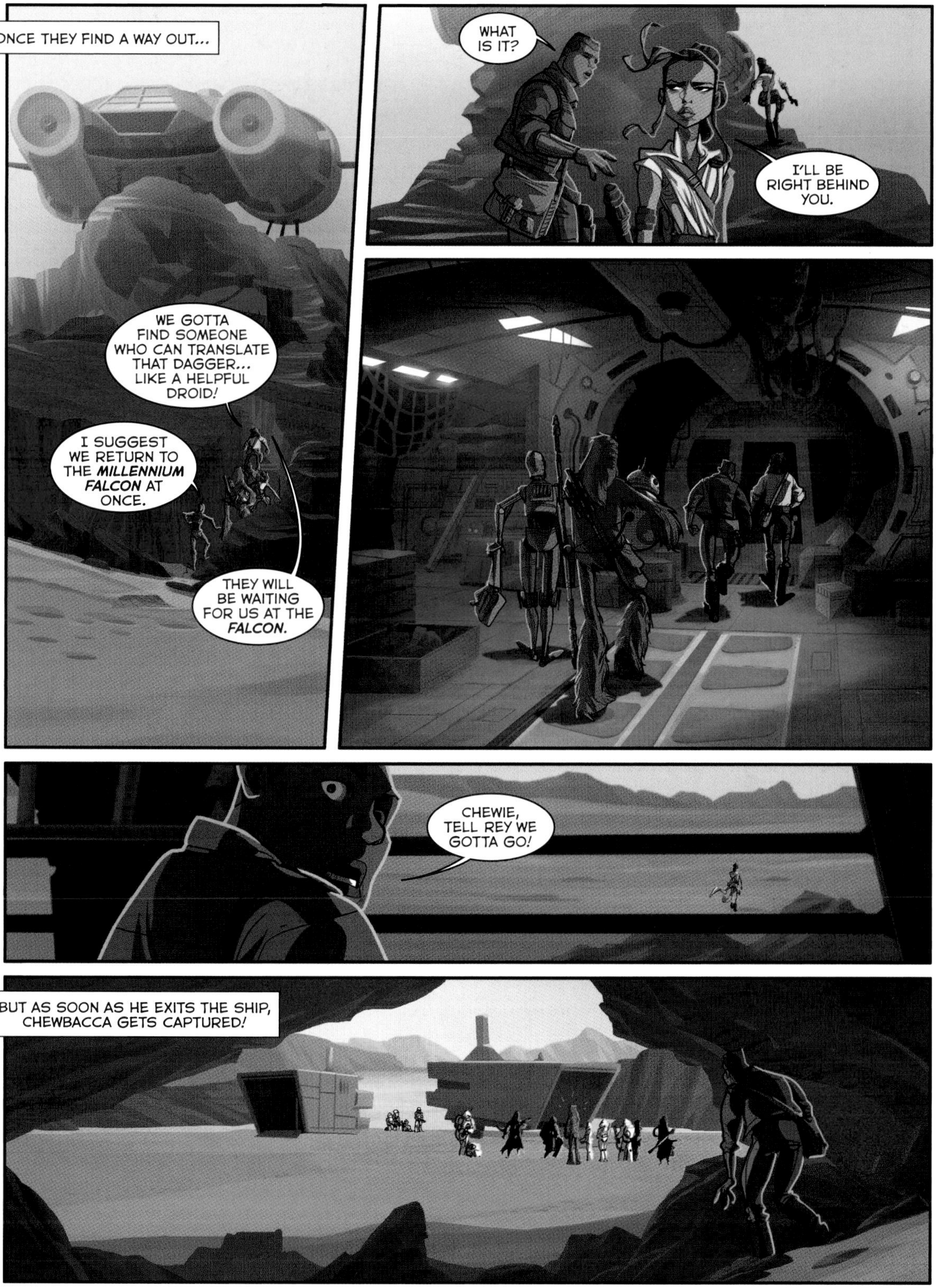
ONCE THEY FIND A WAY OUT...
WHAT IS IT?
I'LL BE RIGHT BEHIND YOU.
WE GOTTA FIND SOMEONE WHO CAN TRANSLATE THAT DAGGER... LIKE A HELPFUL DROID!
I SUGGEST WE RETURN TO THE *MILLENNIUM FALCON* AT ONCE.
THEY WILL BE WAITING FOR US AT THE *FALCON*.
CHEWIE, TELL REY WE GOTTA GO!
BUT AS SOON AS HE EXITS THE SHIP, CHEWBACCA GETS CAPTURED!

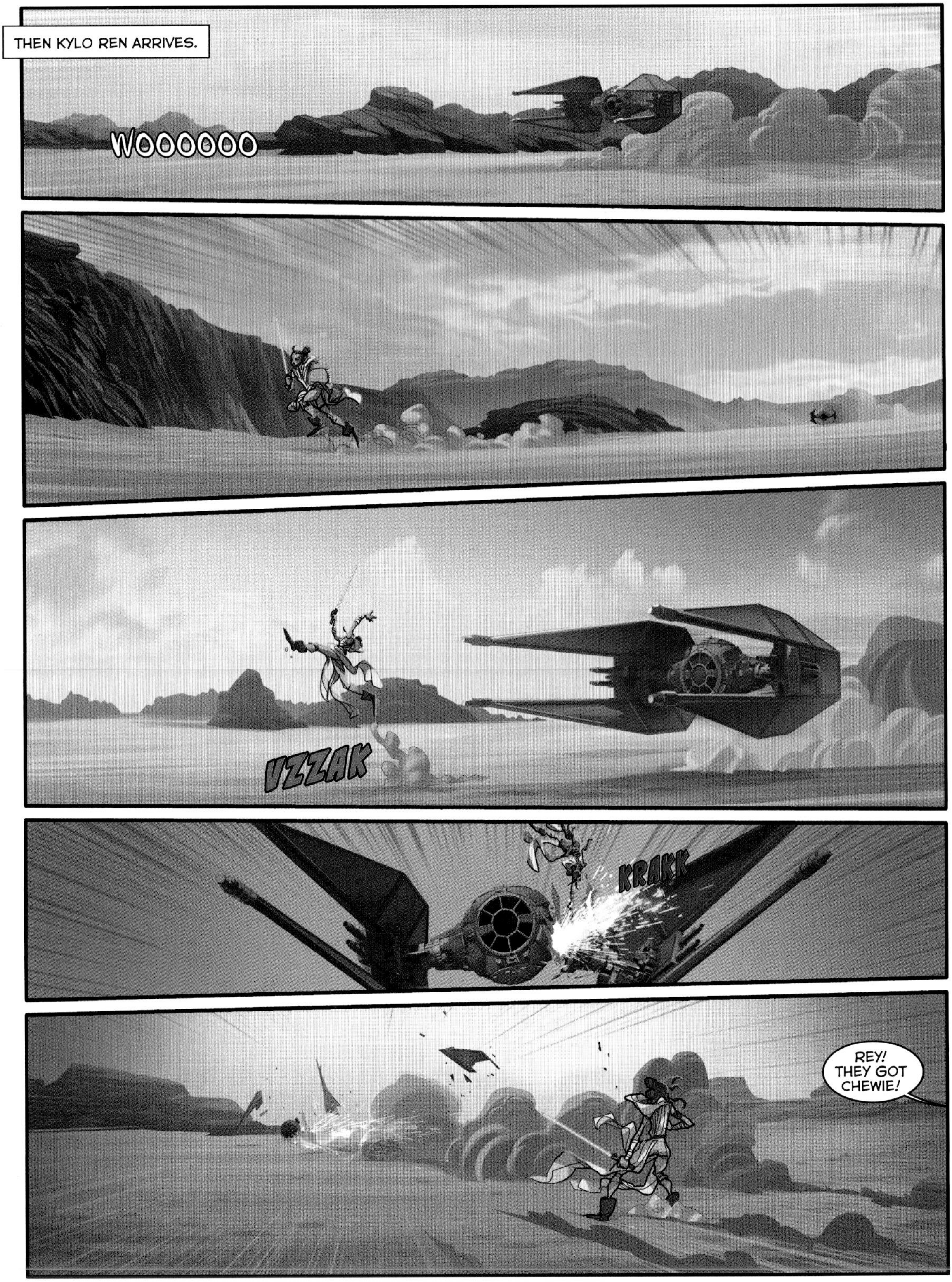
THEN KYLO REN ARRIVES.
WOOOOOO
VZZAK
KRAKK
REY! THEY GOT CHEWIE!

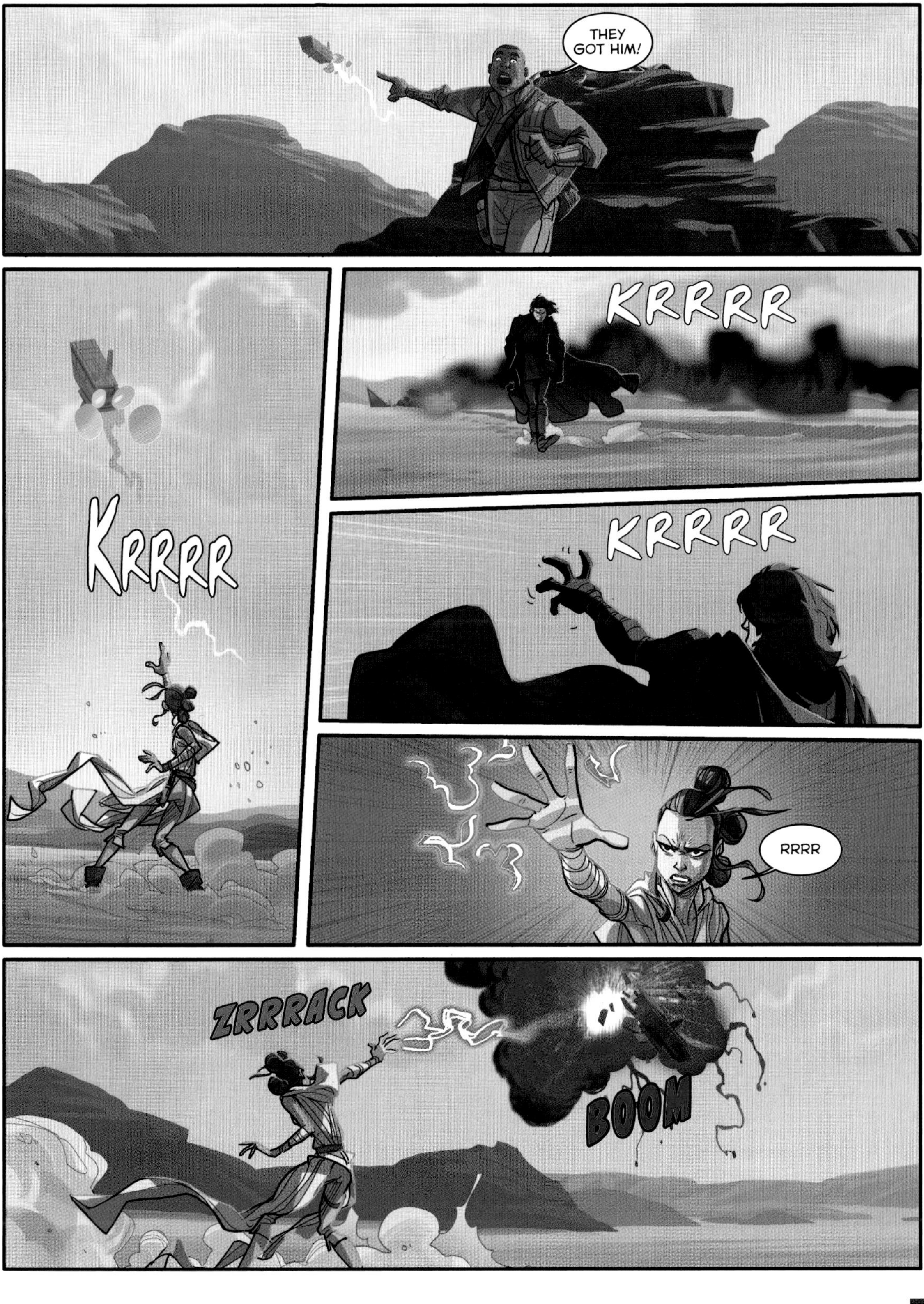

THEY GOT HIM!
KRRRR
KRRRRR
KRRRRR
RRRR
ZRRRACK
BOOM

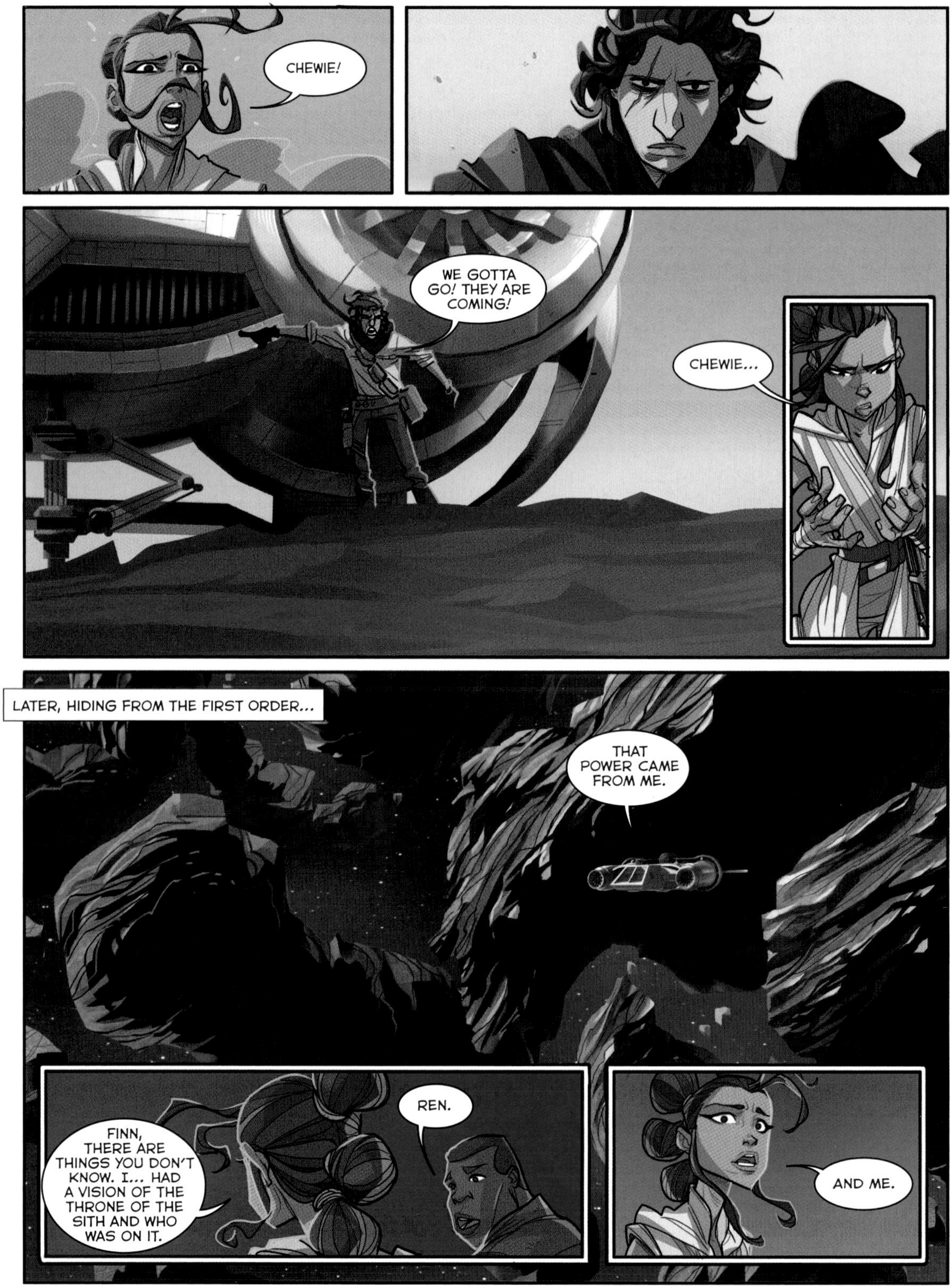
CHEWIE!
WE GOTTA GO! THEY ARE COMING!
CHEWIE...
LATER, HIDING FROM THE FIRST ORDER...
THAT POWER CAME FROM ME.
FINN, THERE ARE THINGS YOU DON'T KNOW. I... HAD A VISION OF THE THRONE OF THE SITH AND WHO WAS ON IT.
REN.
AND ME.

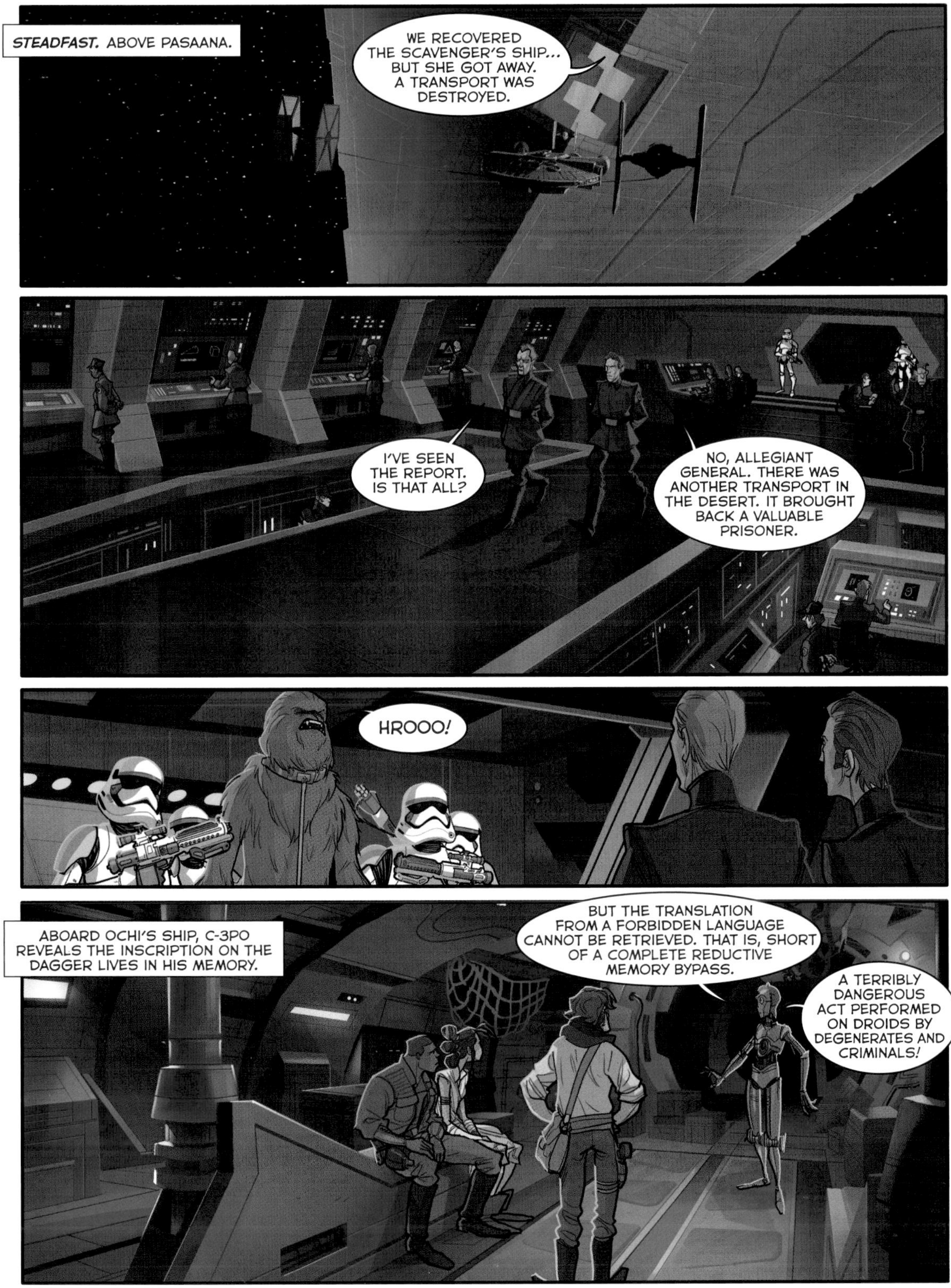

STEADFAST. ABOVE PASAANA.
WE RECOVERED THE SCAVENGER'S SHIP... BUT SHE GOT AWAY. A TRANSPORT WAS DESTROYED.
I'VE SEEN THE REPORT. IS THAT ALL?
NO, ALLEGIANT GENERAL. THERE WAS ANOTHER TRANSPORT IN THE DESERT. IT BROUGHT BACK A VALUABLE PRISONER.
HROOO!
ABOARD OCHI'S SHIP, C-3PO REVEALS THE INSCRIPTION ON THE DAGGER LIVES IN HIS MEMORY.
BUT THE TRANSLATION FROM A FORBIDDEN LANGUAGE CANNOT BE RETRIEVED. THAT IS, SHORT OF A COMPLETE REDUCTIVE MEMORY BYPASS.
A TERRIBLY DANGEROUS ACT PERFORMED ON DROIDS BY DEGENERATES AND CRIMINALS!

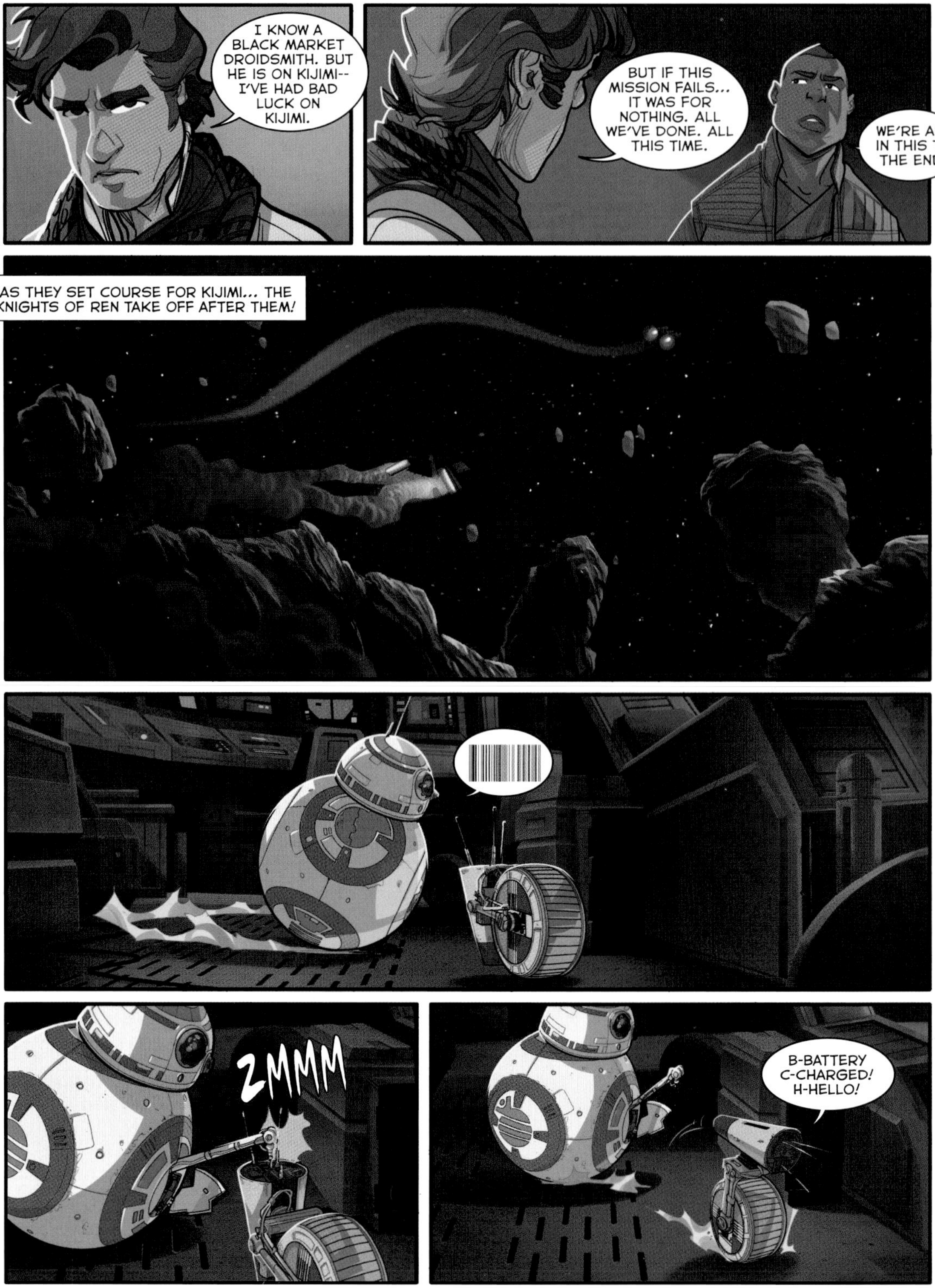
I KNOW A BLACK MARKET DROIDSMITH. BUT HE IS ON KIJIMI-- I'VE HAD BAD LUCK ON KIJIMI.
BUT IF THIS MISSION FAILS... IT WAS FOR NOTHING. ALL WE'VE DONE. ALL THIS TIME.
WE'RE ALL IN THIS TO THE END.
AS THEY SET COURSE FOR KIJIMI... THE KNIGHTS OF REN TAKE OFF AFTER THEM!
ZMMM
B-BATTERY C-CHARGED! H-HELLO!

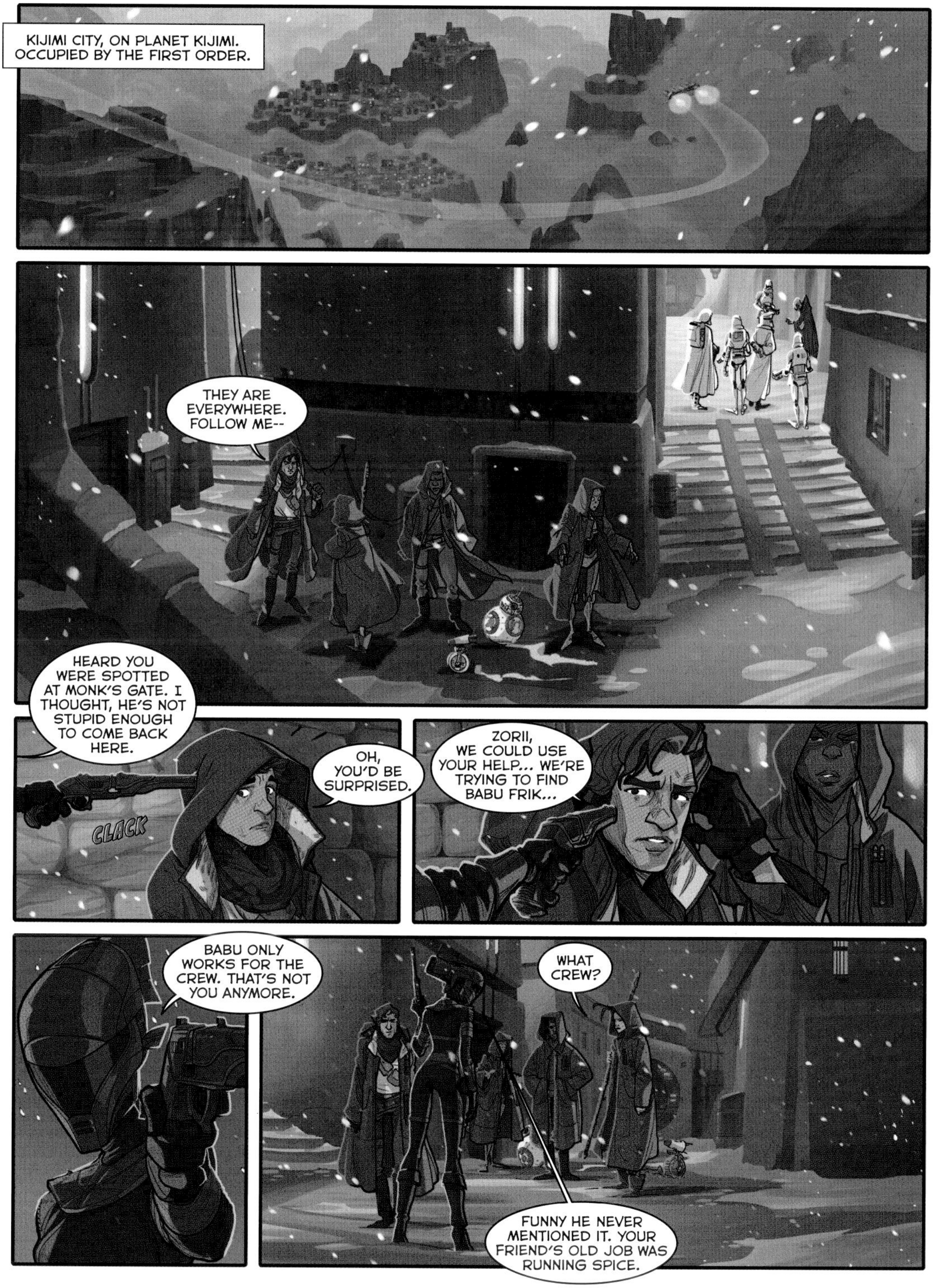

KIJIMI CITY, ON PLANET KIJIMI. OCCUPIED BY THE FIRST ORDER.
THEY ARE EVERYWHERE. FOLLOW ME--
HEARD YOU WERE SPOTTED AT MONK'S GATE. I THOUGHT, HE'S NOT STUPID ENOUGH TO COME BACK HERE.
CLACK
OH, YOU'D BE SURPRISED.
ZORII, WE COULD USE YOUR HELP... WE'RE TRYING TO FIND BABU FRIK...
BABU ONLY WORKS FOR THE CREW. THAT'S NOT YOU ANYMORE.
WHAT CREW?
FUNNY HE NEVER MENTIONED IT. YOUR FRIEND'S OLD JOB WAS RUNNING SPICE.

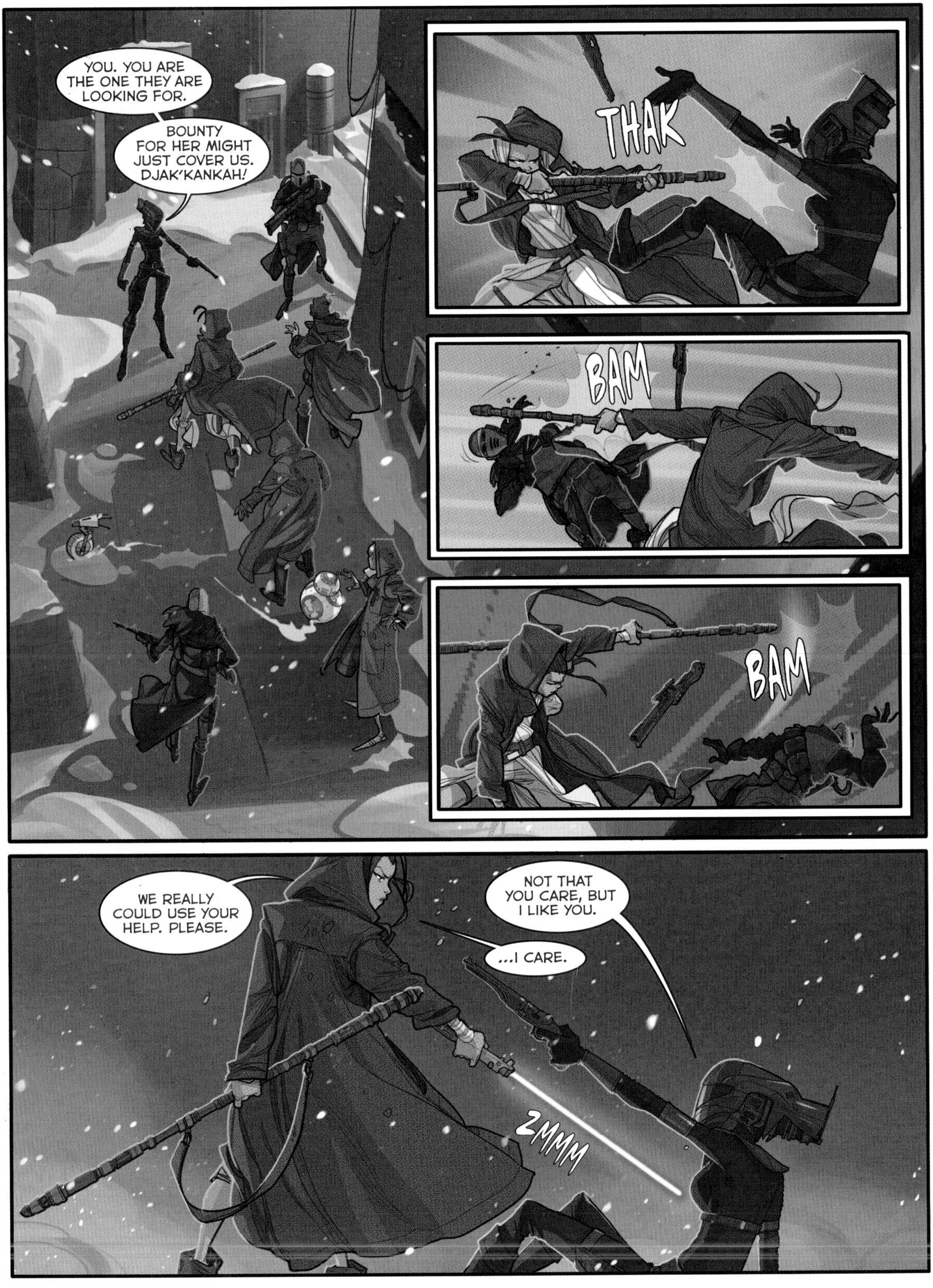
YOU. YOU ARE THE ONE THEY ARE LOOKING FOR.
BOUNTY FOR HER MIGHT JUST COVER US. DJAK'KANKAH!
THAK
BAM
BAM
WE REALLY COULD USE YOUR HELP. PLEASE.
NOT THAT YOU CARE, BUT I LIKE YOU.
...I CARE.
ZMMM

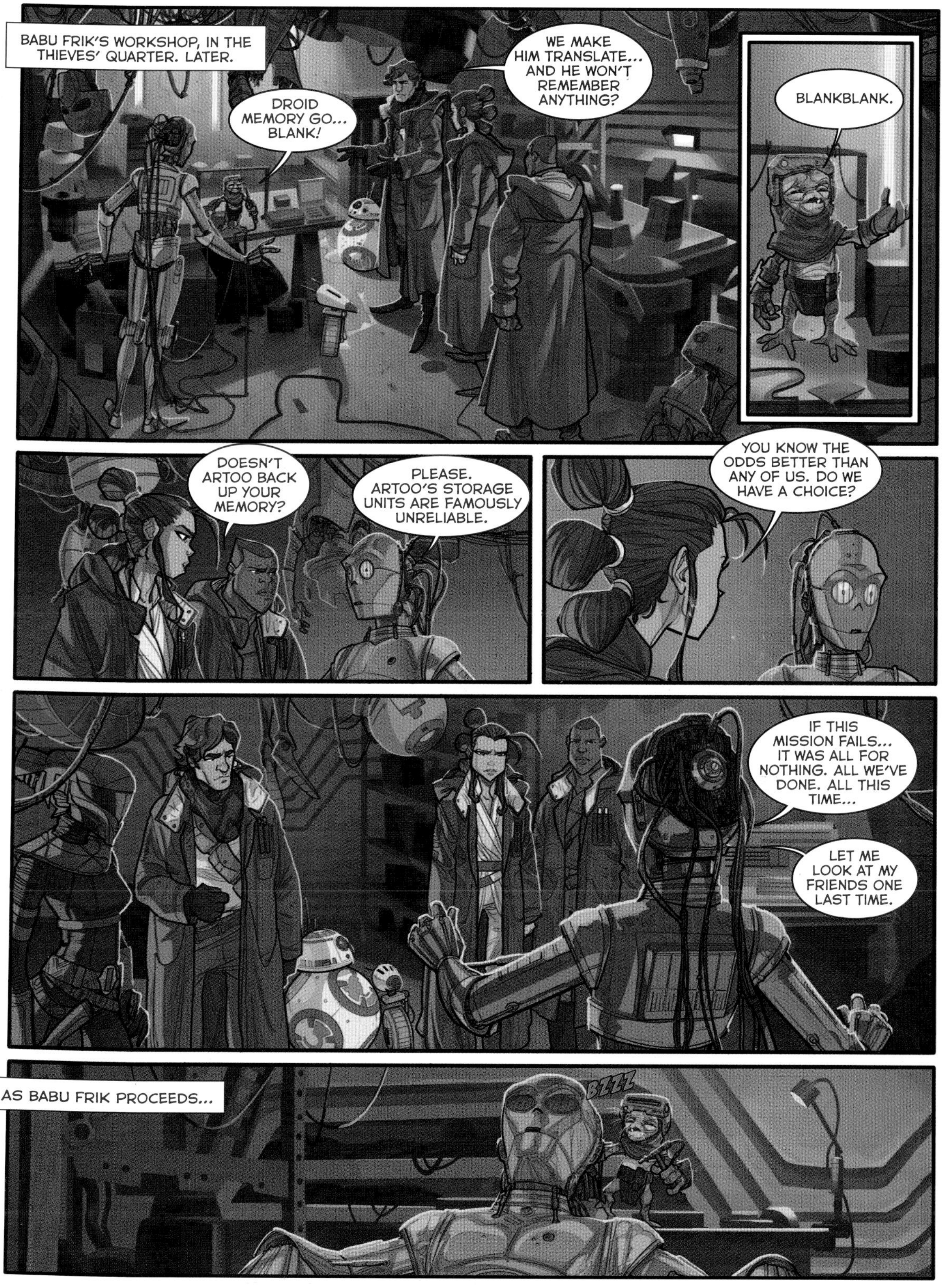

BABU FRIK'S WORKSHOP, IN THE THIEVES' QUARTER. LATER.
DROID MEMORY GO... BLANK!
WE MAKE HIM TRANSLATE... AND HE WON'T REMEMBER ANYTHING?
BLANKBLANK.
DOESN'T ARTOO BACK UP YOUR MEMORY?
PLEASE. ARTOO'S STORAGE UNITS ARE FAMOUSLY UNRELIABLE.
YOU KNOW THE ODDS BETTER THAN ANY OF US. DO WE HAVE A CHOICE?
IF THIS MISSION FAILS... IT WAS ALL FOR NOTHING. ALL WE'VE DONE. ALL THIS TIME...
LET ME LOOK AT MY FRIENDS ONE LAST TIME.
AS BABU FRIK PROCEEDS...
BZZZ

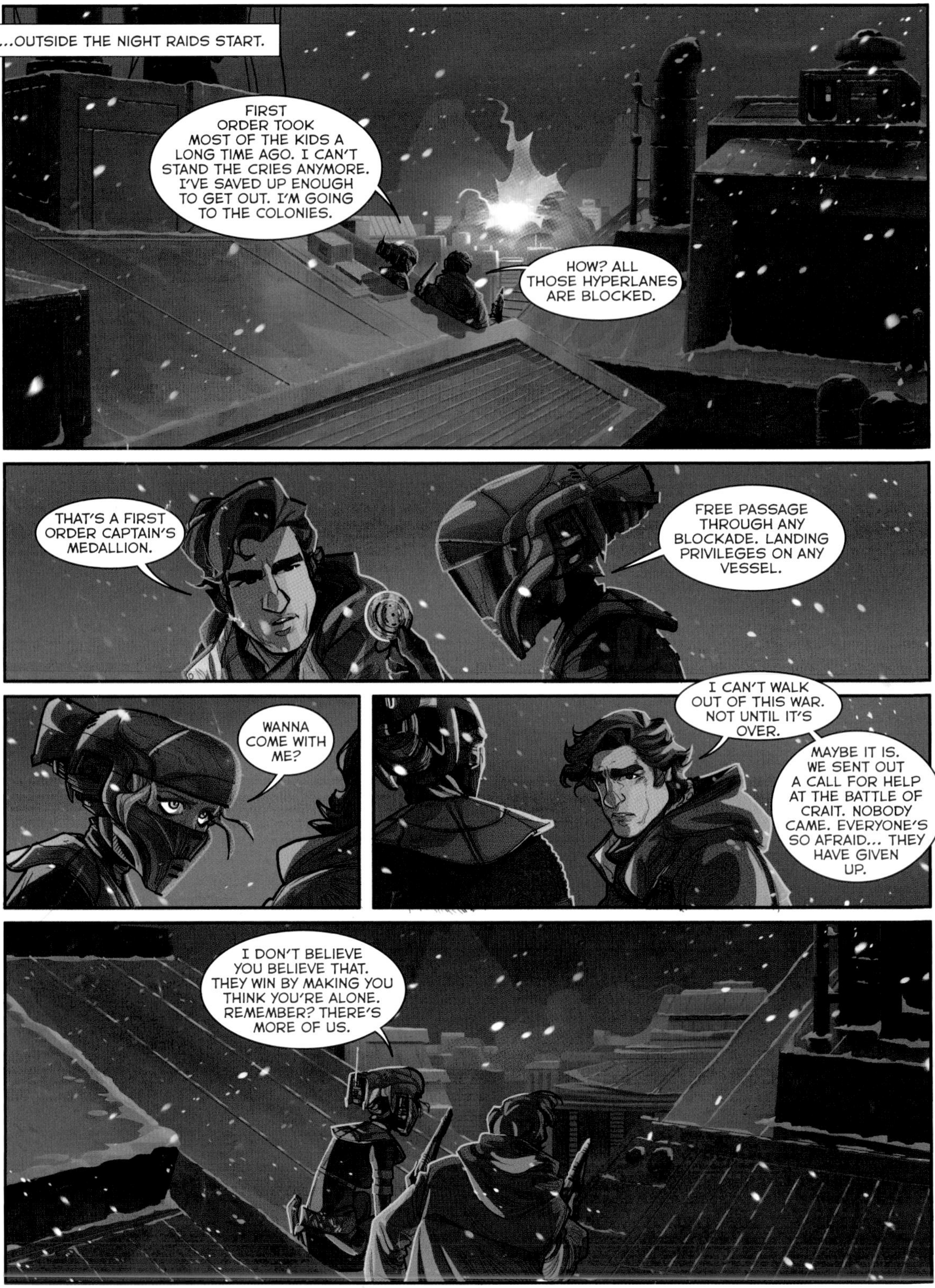

...OUTSIDE THE NIGHT RAIDS START.
FIRST ORDER TOOK MOST OF THE KIDS A LONG TIME AGO. I CAN'T STAND THE CRIES ANYMORE. I'VE SAVED UP ENOUGH TO GET OUT. I'M GOING TO THE COLONIES.
HOW? ALL THOSE HYPERLANES ARE BLOCKED.
THAT'S A FIRST ORDER CAPTAIN'S MEDALLION.
FREE PASSAGE THROUGH ANY BLOCKADE. LANDING PRIVILEGES ON ANY VESSEL.
WANNA COME WITH ME?
I CAN'T WALK OUT OF THIS WAR. NOT UNTIL IT'S OVER.
MAYBE IT IS. WE SENT OUT A CALL FOR HELP AT THE BATTLE OF CRAIT. NOBODY CAME. EVERYONE'S SO AFRAID... THEY HAVE GIVEN UP.
I DON'T BELIEVE YOU BELIEVE THAT. THEY WIN BY MAKING YOU THINK YOU'RE ALONE. REMEMBER? THERE'S MORE OF US.

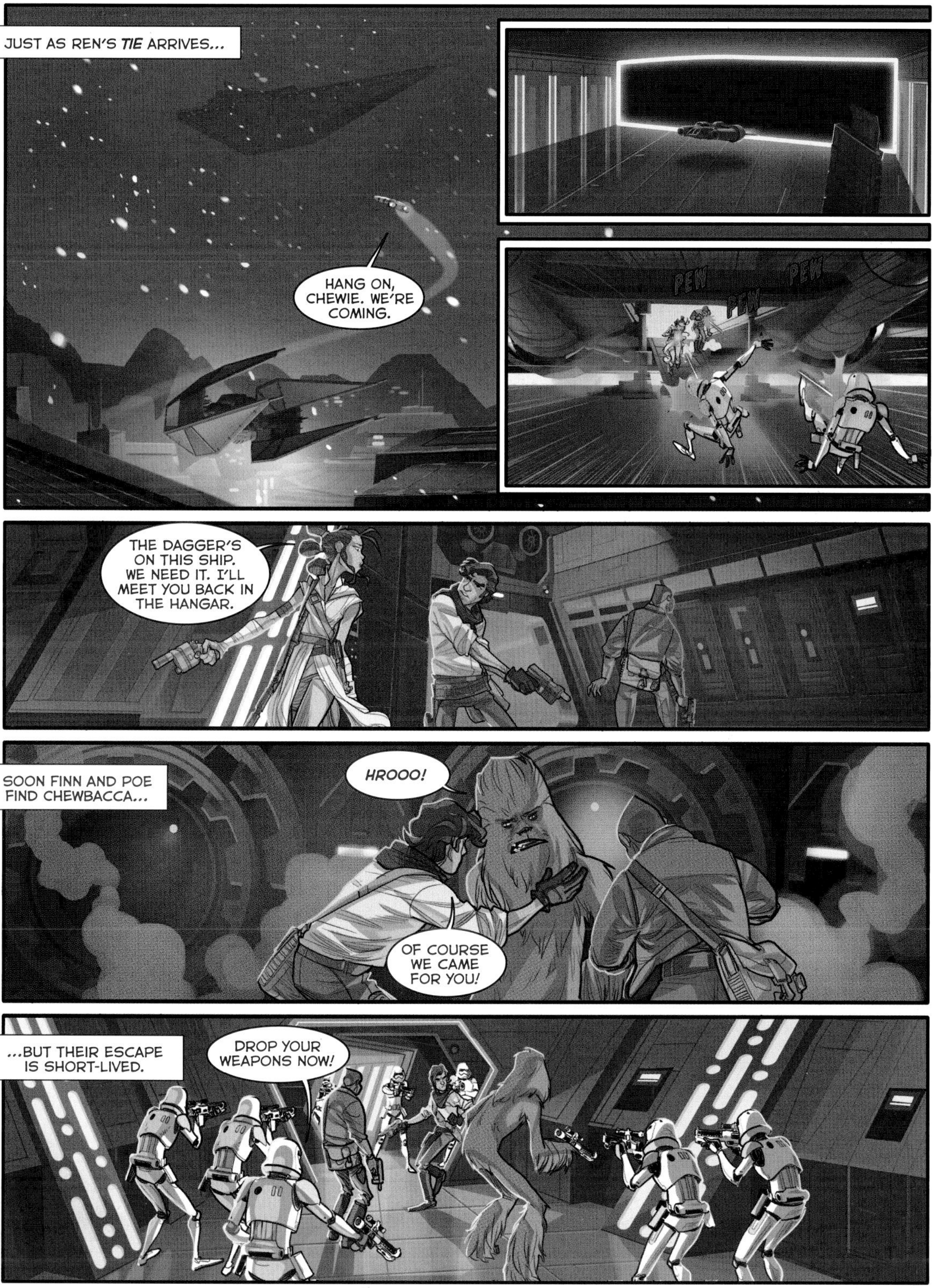
JUST AS REN'S TIE ARRIVES...
HANG ON, CHEWIE. WE'RE COMING.
PEW
PEW
PEW
THE DAGGER'S ON THIS SHIP. WE NEED IT. I'LL MEET YOU BACK IN THE HANGAR.
SOON FINN AND POE FIND CHEWBACCA...
HROOO!
OF COURSE WE CAME FOR YOU!
...BUT THEIR ESCAPE IS SHORT-LIVED.
DROP YOUR WEAPONS NOW!

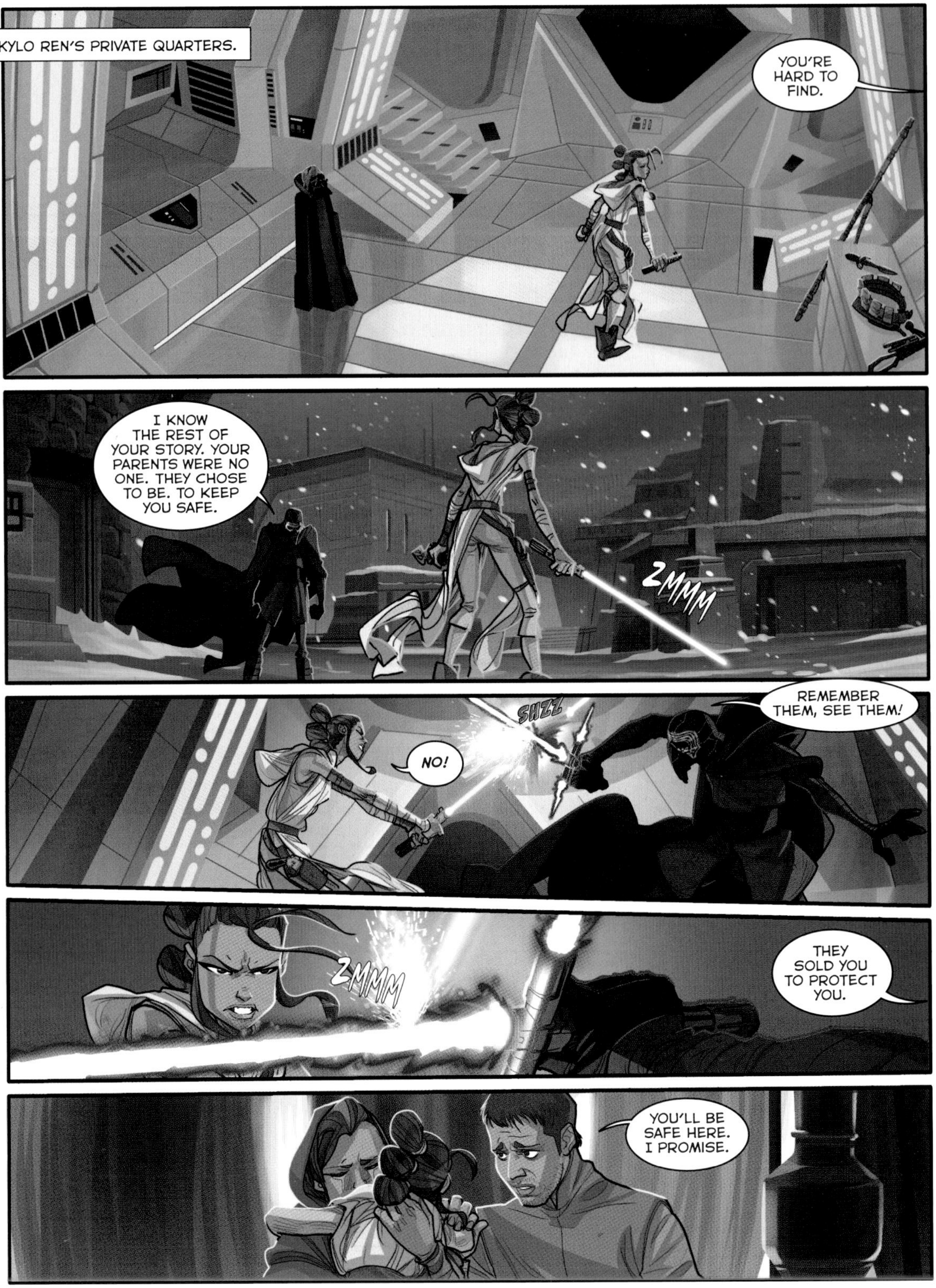
KYLO REN'S PRIVATE QUARTERS.
YOU'RE HARD TO FIND.
I KNOW THE REST OF YOUR STORY. YOUR PARENTS WERE NO ONE. THEY CHOSE TO BE. TO KEEP YOU SAFE.
ZMMM
REMEMBER THEM, SEE THEM!
SHZZ
NO!
ZMMM
THEY SOLD YOU TO PROTECT YOU.
YOU'LL BE SAFE HERE. I PROMISE.

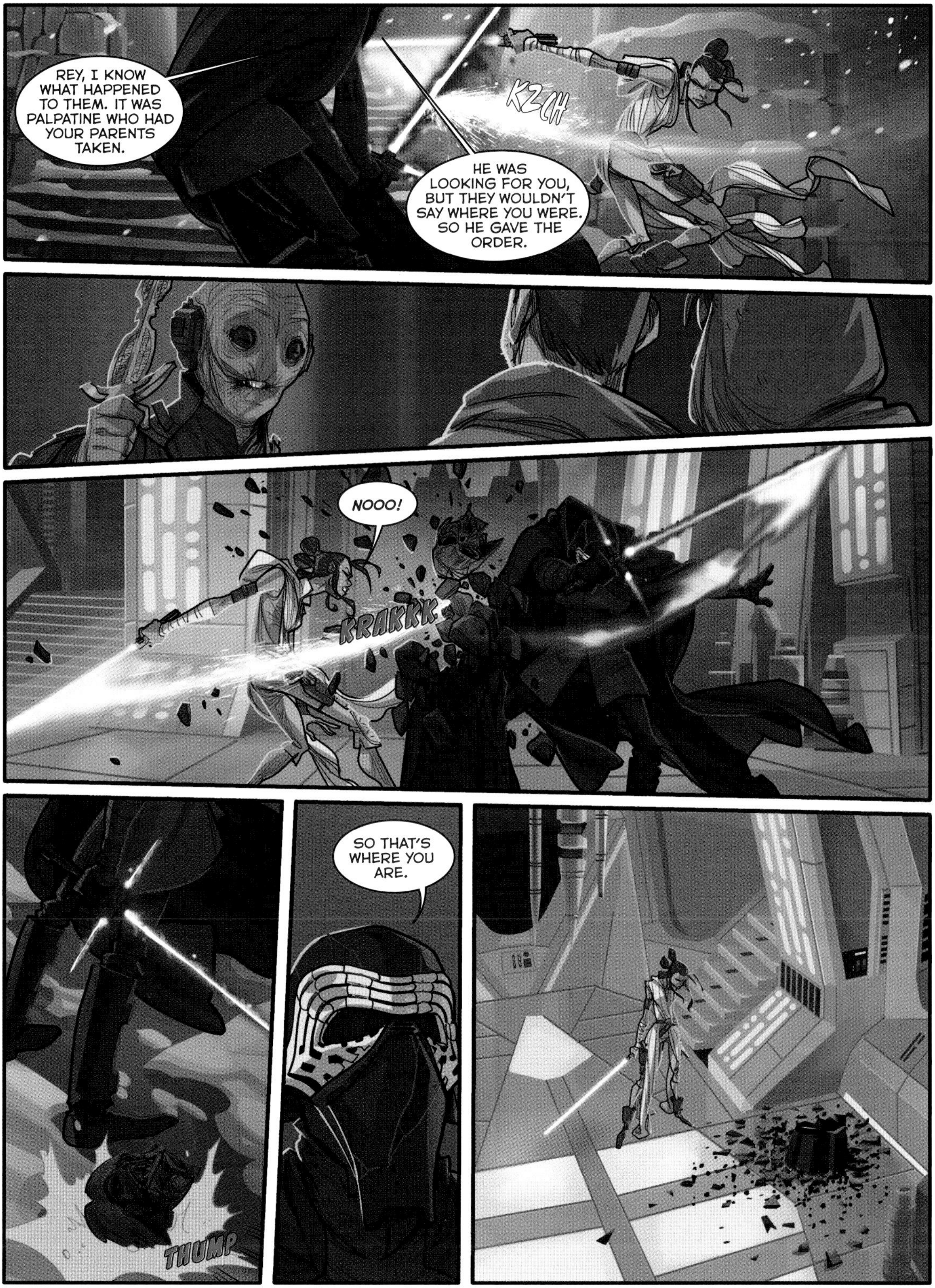

REY, I KNOW WHAT HAPPENED TO THEM. IT WAS PALPATINE WHO HAD YOUR PARENTS TAKEN.
K2CH
HE WAS LOOKING FOR YOU, BUT THEY WOULDN'T SAY WHERE YOU WERE. SO HE GAVE THE ORDER.
NOOO!
KRAKKK
THUMP
SO THAT'S WHERE YOU ARE.

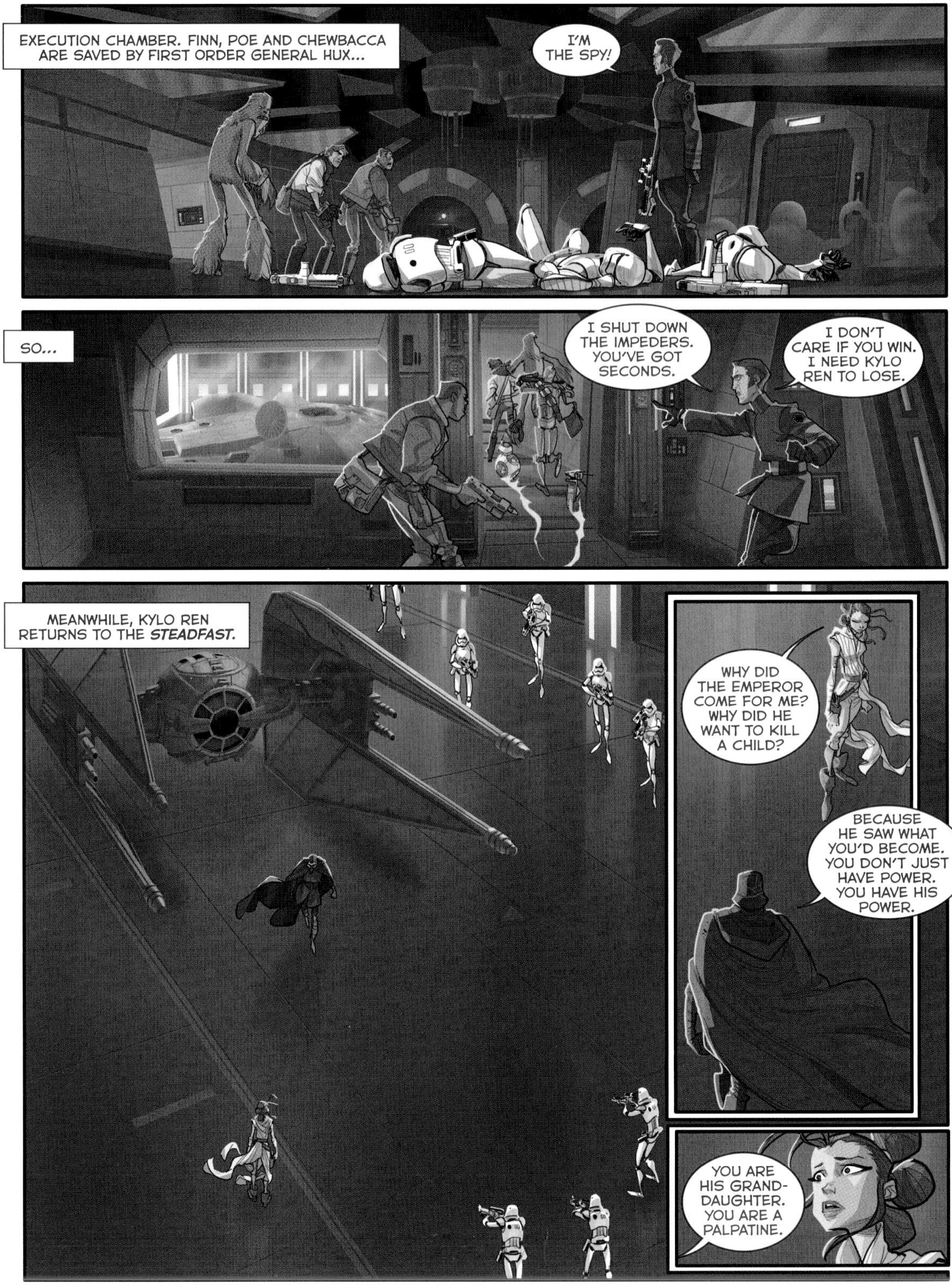

EXECUTION CHAMBER. FINN, POE AND CHEWBACCA ARE SAVED BY FIRST ORDER GENERAL HUX...
I'M THE SPY!
SO...
I SHUT DOWN THE IMPEDERS. YOU'VE GOT SECONDS.
I DON'T CARE IF YOU WIN. I NEED KYLO REN TO LOSE.
MEANWHILE, KYLO REN RETURNS TO THE *STEADFAST*.
WHY DID THE EMPEROR COME FOR ME? WHY DID HE WANT TO KILL A CHILD?
BECAUSE HE SAW WHAT YOU'D BECOME. YOU DON'T JUST HAVE POWER. YOU HAVE HIS POWER.
YOU ARE HIS GRAND-DAUGHTER. YOU ARE A PALPATINE.

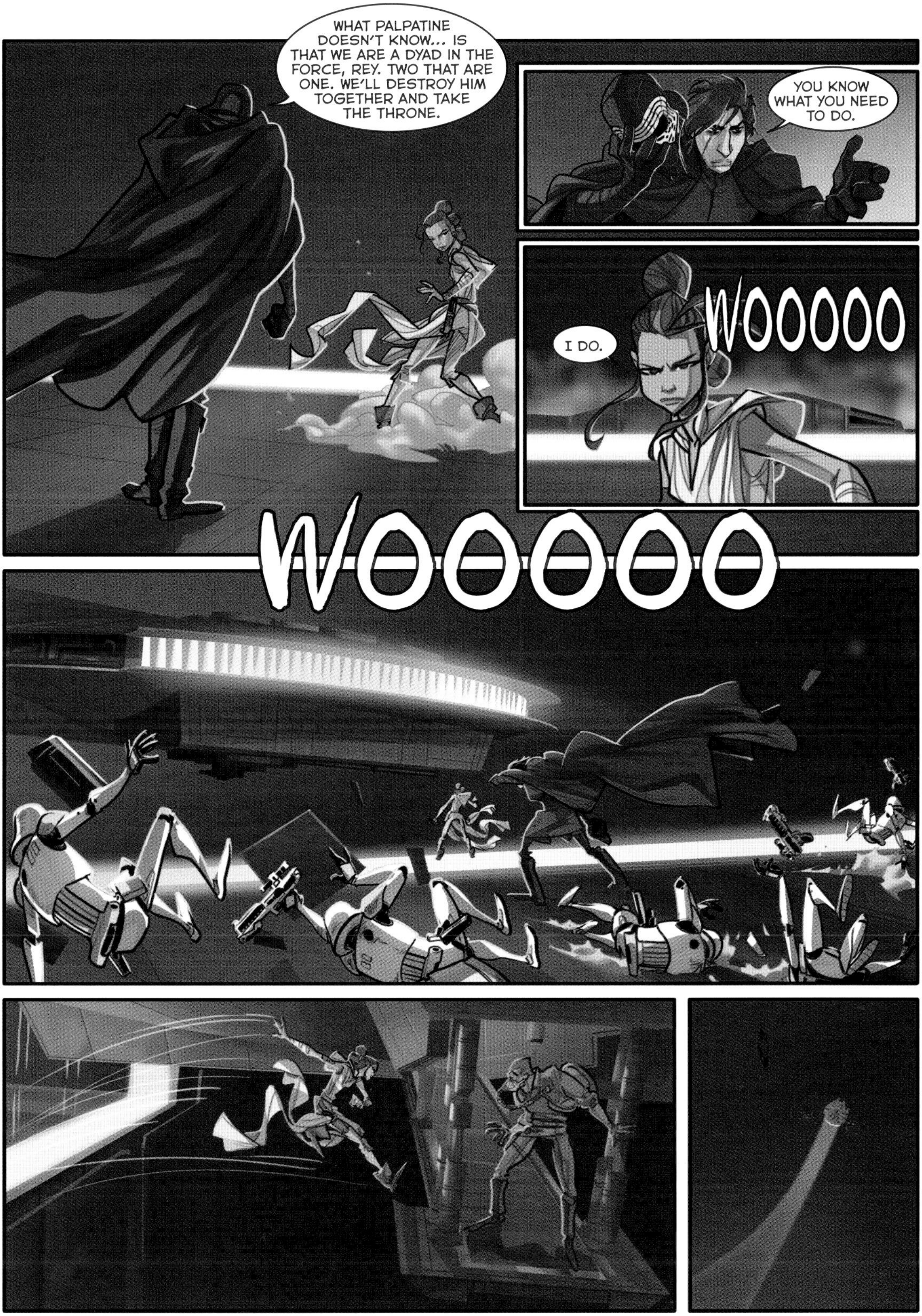

WHAT PALPATINE DOESN'T KNOW... IS THAT WE ARE A DYAD IN THE FORCE, REY. TWO THAT ARE ONE. WE'LL DESTROY HIM TOGETHER AND TAKE THE THRONE.
YOU KNOW WHAT YOU NEED TO DO.
I DO.
WOOOOO
WOOOOO

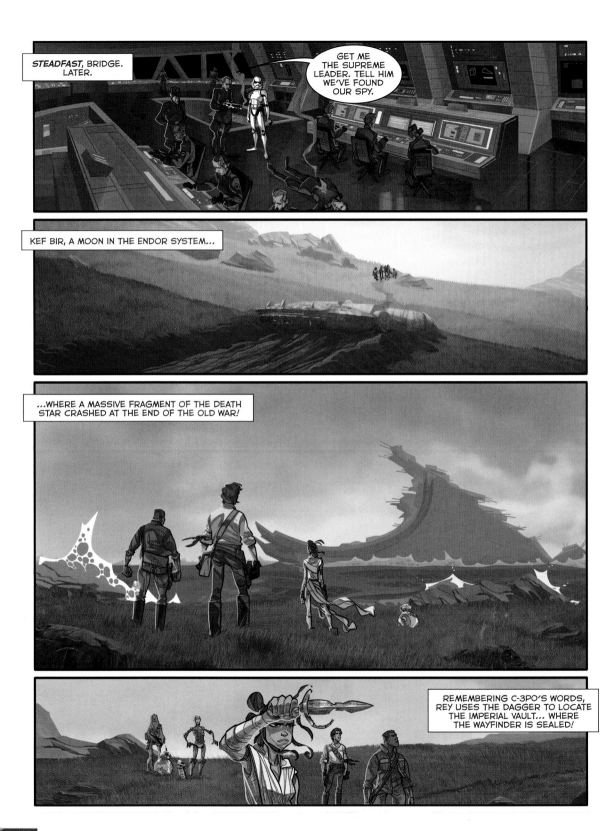

STEADFAST, BRIDGE. LATER.

GET ME THE SUPREME LEADER. TELL HIM WE'VE FOUND OUR SPY.

KEF BIR, A MOON IN THE ENDOR SYSTEM...

...WHERE A MASSIVE FRAGMENT OF THE DEATH STAR CRASHED AT THE END OF THE OLD WAR!

REMEMBERING C-3PO'S WORDS, REY USES THE DAGGER TO LOCATE THE IMPERIAL VAULT... WHERE THE WAYFINDER IS SEALED!

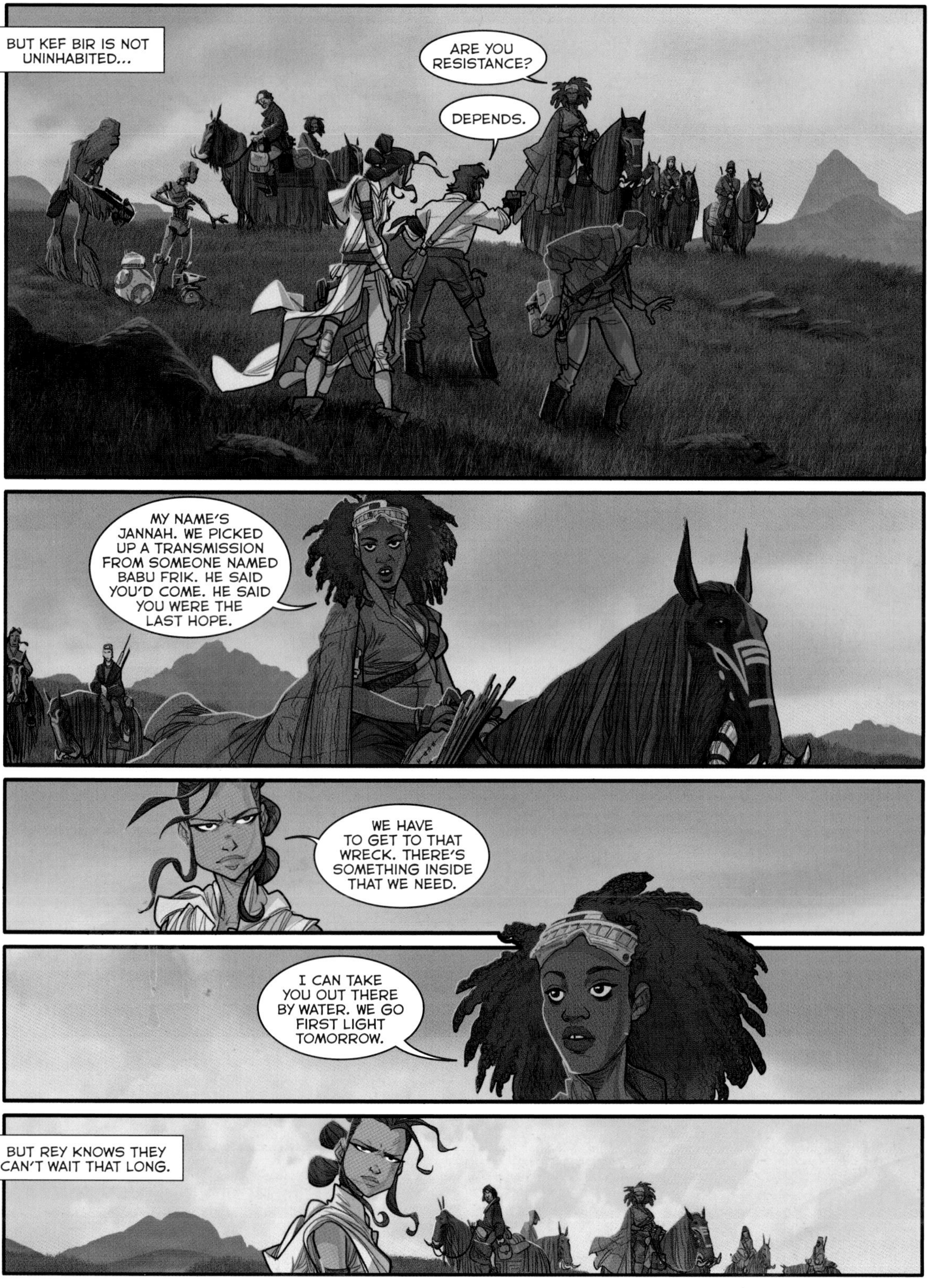

BUT KEF BIR IS NOT UNINHABITED...
ARE YOU RESISTANCE?
DEPENDS.
MY NAME'S JANNAH. WE PICKED UP A TRANSMISSION FROM SOMEONE NAMED BABU FRIK. HE SAID YOU'D COME. HE SAID YOU WERE THE LAST HOPE.
WE HAVE TO GET TO THAT WRECK. THERE'S SOMETHING INSIDE THAT WE NEED.
I CAN TAKE YOU OUT THERE BY WATER. WE GO FIRST LIGHT TOMORROW.
BUT REY KNOWS THEY CAN'T WAIT THAT LONG.

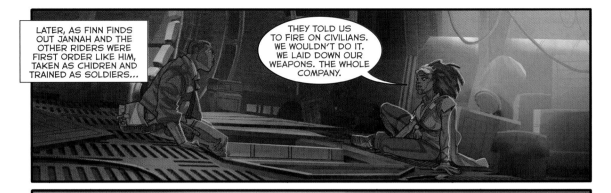

LATER, AS FINN FINDS OUT JANNAH AND THE OTHER RIDERS WERE FIRST ORDER LIKE HIM, TAKEN AS CHIDREN AND TRAINED AS SOLDIERS...

THEY TOLD US TO FIRE ON CIVILIANS. WE WOULDN'T DO IT. WE LAID DOWN OUR WEAPONS. THE WHOLE COMPANY.

...REY TAKES A SKIMMER AND GOES ALONE!

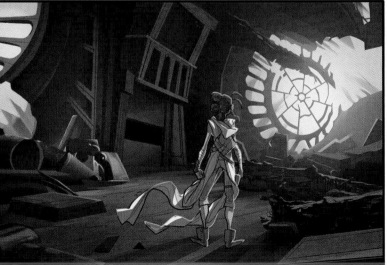

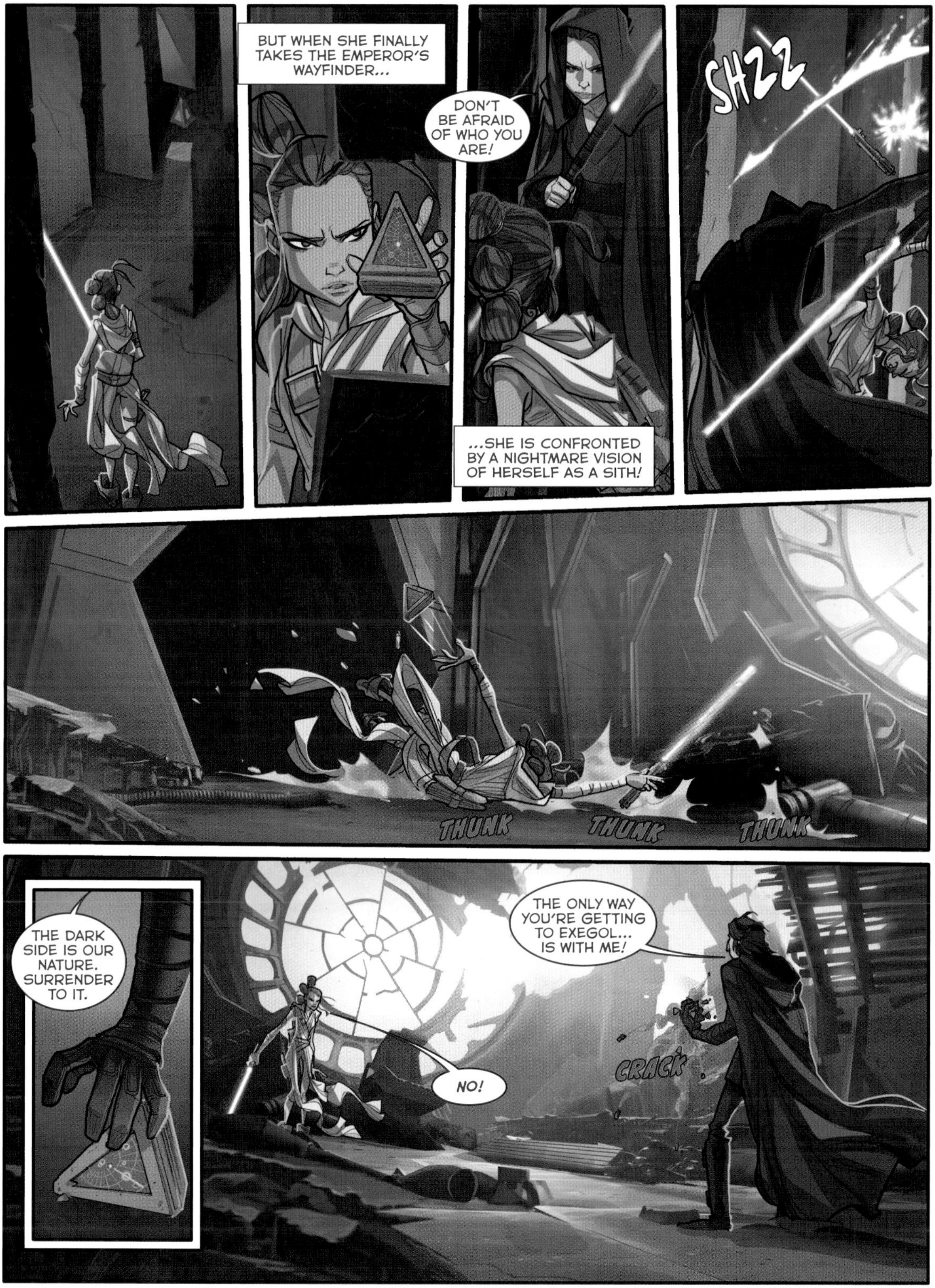
BUT WHEN SHE FINALLY TAKES THE EMPEROR'S WAYFINDER...
DON'T BE AFRAID OF WHO YOU ARE!
...SHE IS CONFRONTED BY A NIGHTMARE VISION OF HERSELF AS A SITH!
SHZZ
THUNK
THUNK
THUNK
THE DARK SIDE IS OUR NATURE. SURRENDER TO IT.
THE ONLY WAY YOU'RE GETTING TO EXEGOL... IS WITH ME!
CRACK
NO!

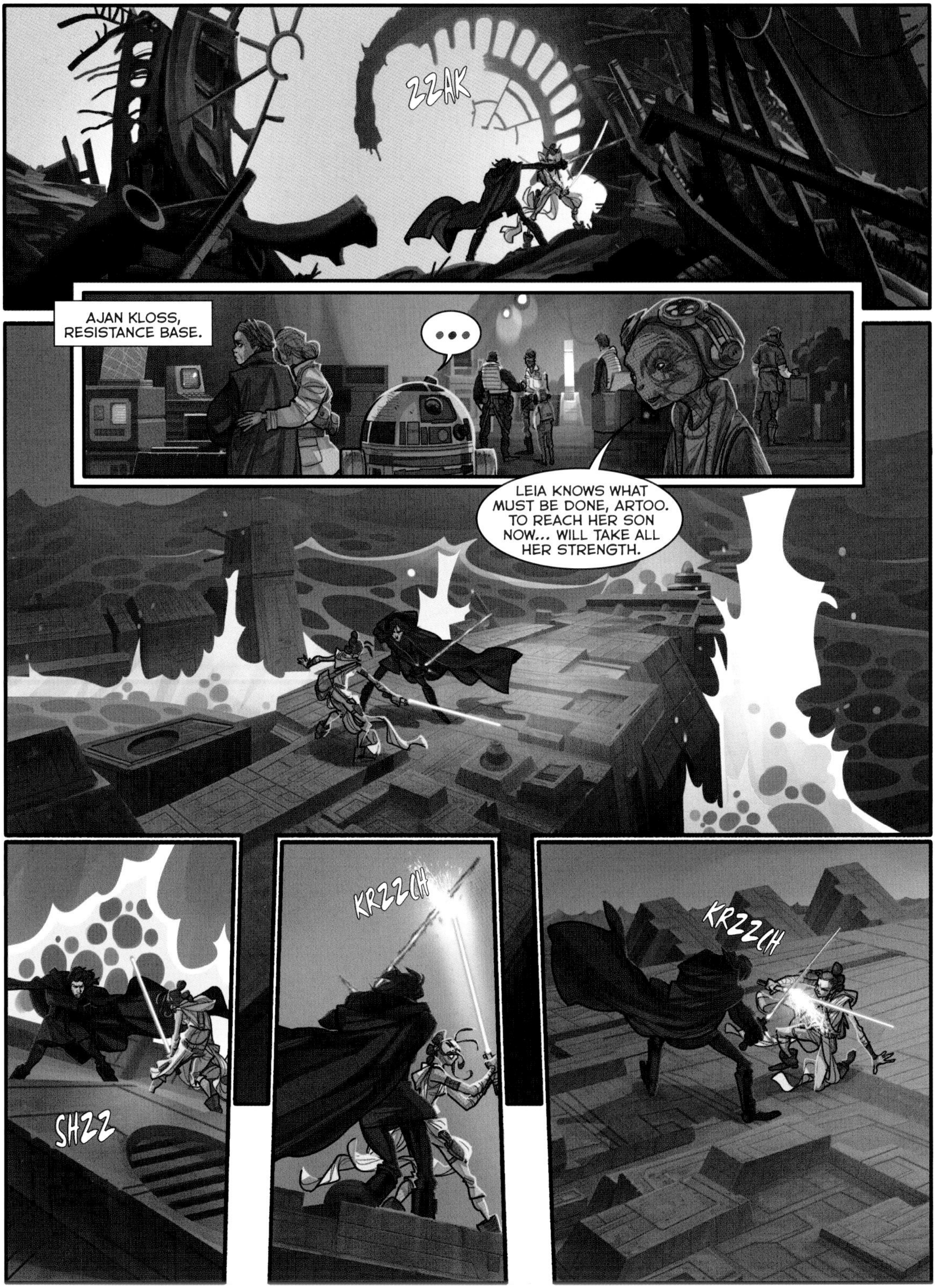
ZZAK
AJAN KLOSS, RESISTANCE BASE.
...
LEIA KNOWS WHAT MUST BE DONE, ARTOO. TO REACH HER SON NOW... WILL TAKE ALL HER STRENGTH.
SHZZ
KRZZCH
KRZZCH

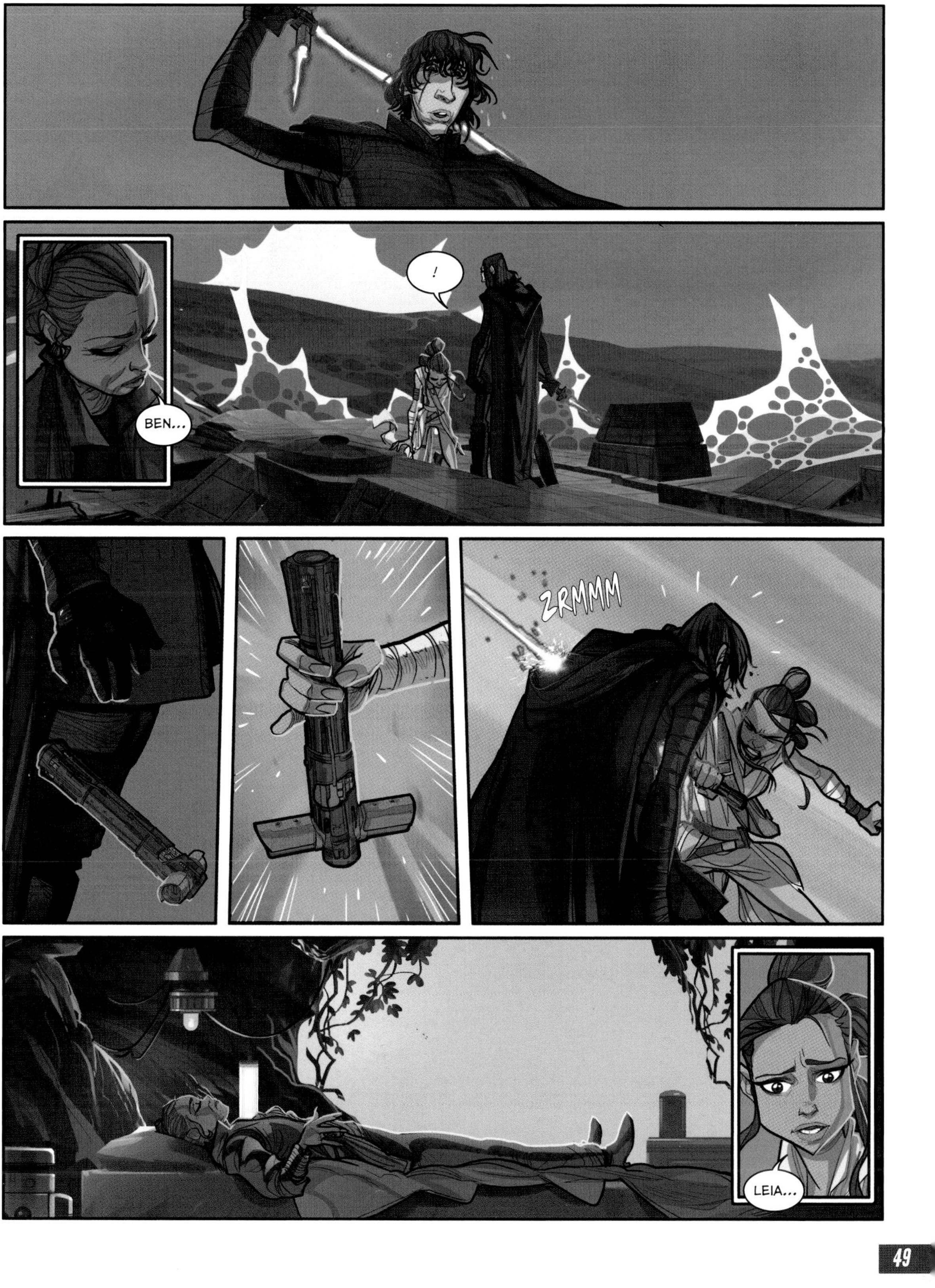
BEN...
!
ZRMMM
LEIA...

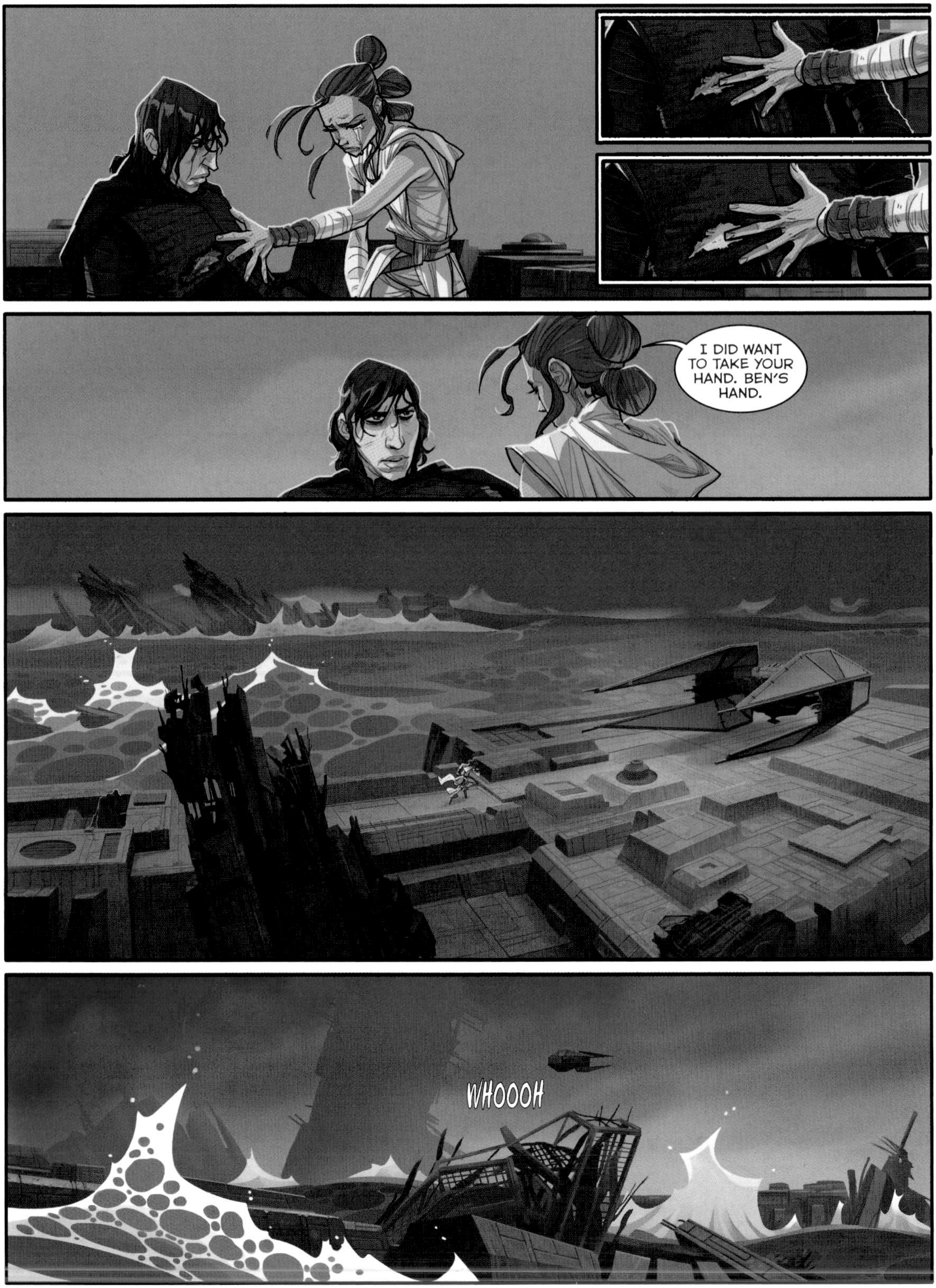
I DID WANT TO TAKE YOUR HAND. BEN'S HAND.
WHOOOH

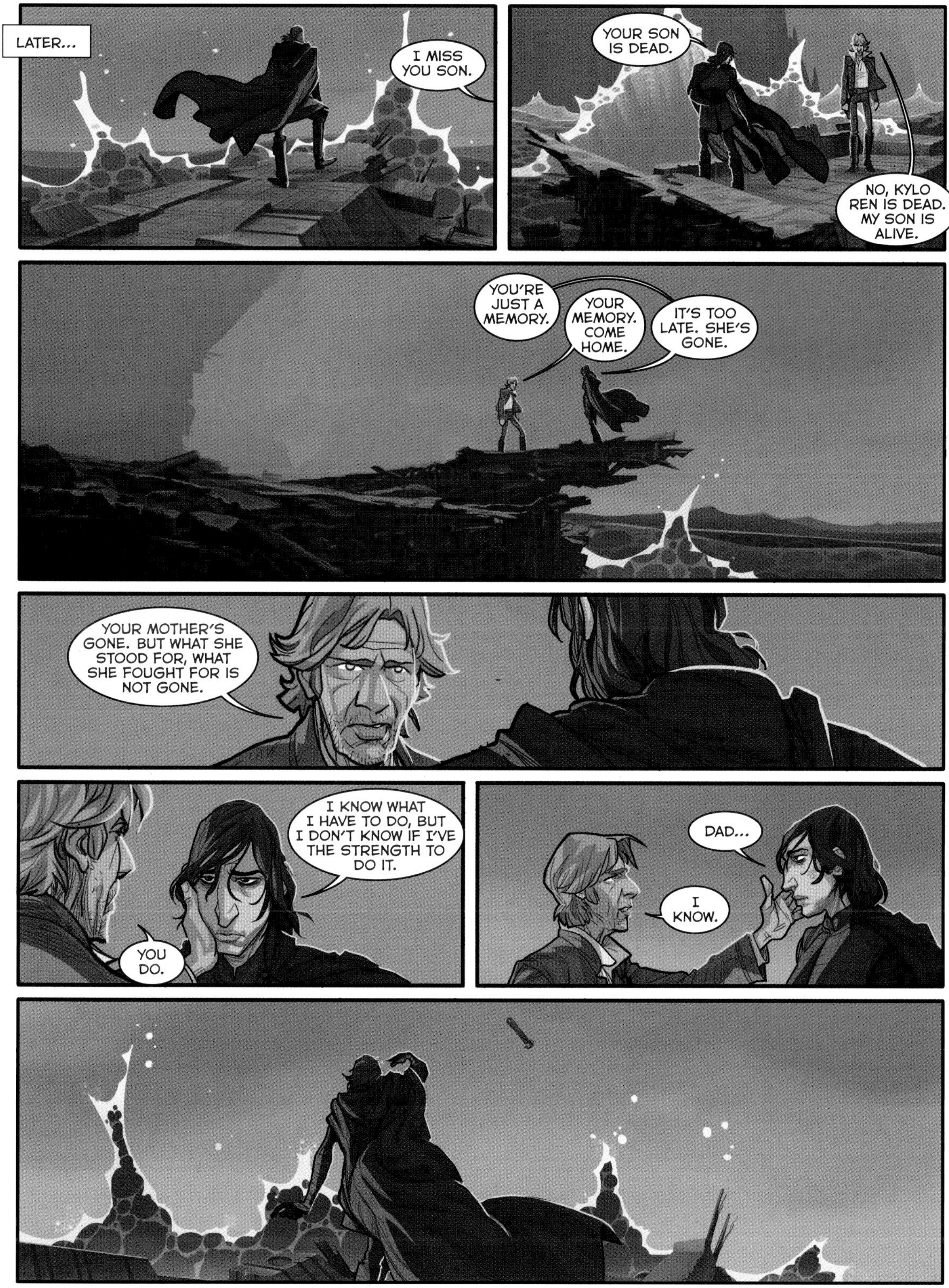
LATER...
I MISS YOU SON.
YOUR SON IS DEAD.
NO, KYLO REN IS DEAD. MY SON IS ALIVE.
YOU'RE JUST A MEMORY.
YOUR MEMORY. COME HOME.
IT'S TOO LATE. SHE'S GONE.
YOUR MOTHER'S GONE. BUT WHAT SHE STOOD FOR, WHAT SHE FOUGHT FOR IS NOT GONE.
I KNOW WHAT I HAVE TO DO, BUT I DON'T KNOW IF I'VE THE STRENGTH TO DO IT.
YOU DO.
DAD...
I KNOW.

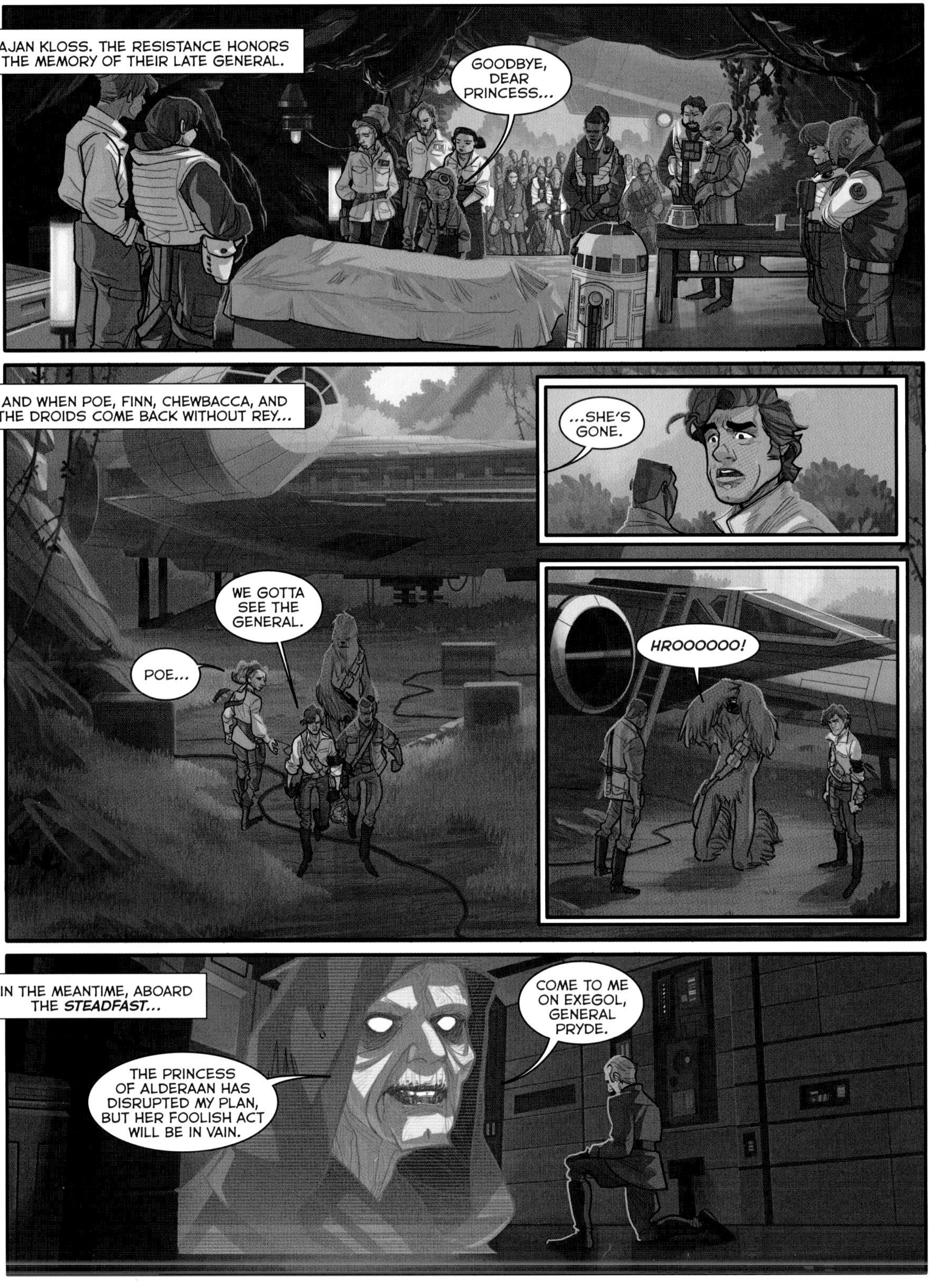
AJAN KLOSS. THE RESISTANCE HONORS THE MEMORY OF THEIR LATE GENERAL.
GOODBYE, DEAR PRINCESS...
AND WHEN POE, FINN, CHEWBACCA, AND THE DROIDS COME BACK WITHOUT REY...
WE GOTTA SEE THE GENERAL.
POE...
...SHE'S GONE.
HROOOOOO!
IN THE MEANTIME, ABOARD THE *STEADFAST*...
THE PRINCESS OF ALDERAAN HAS DISRUPTED MY PLAN, BUT HER FOOLISH ACT WILL BE IN VAIN.
COME TO ME ON EXEGOL, GENERAL PRYDE.

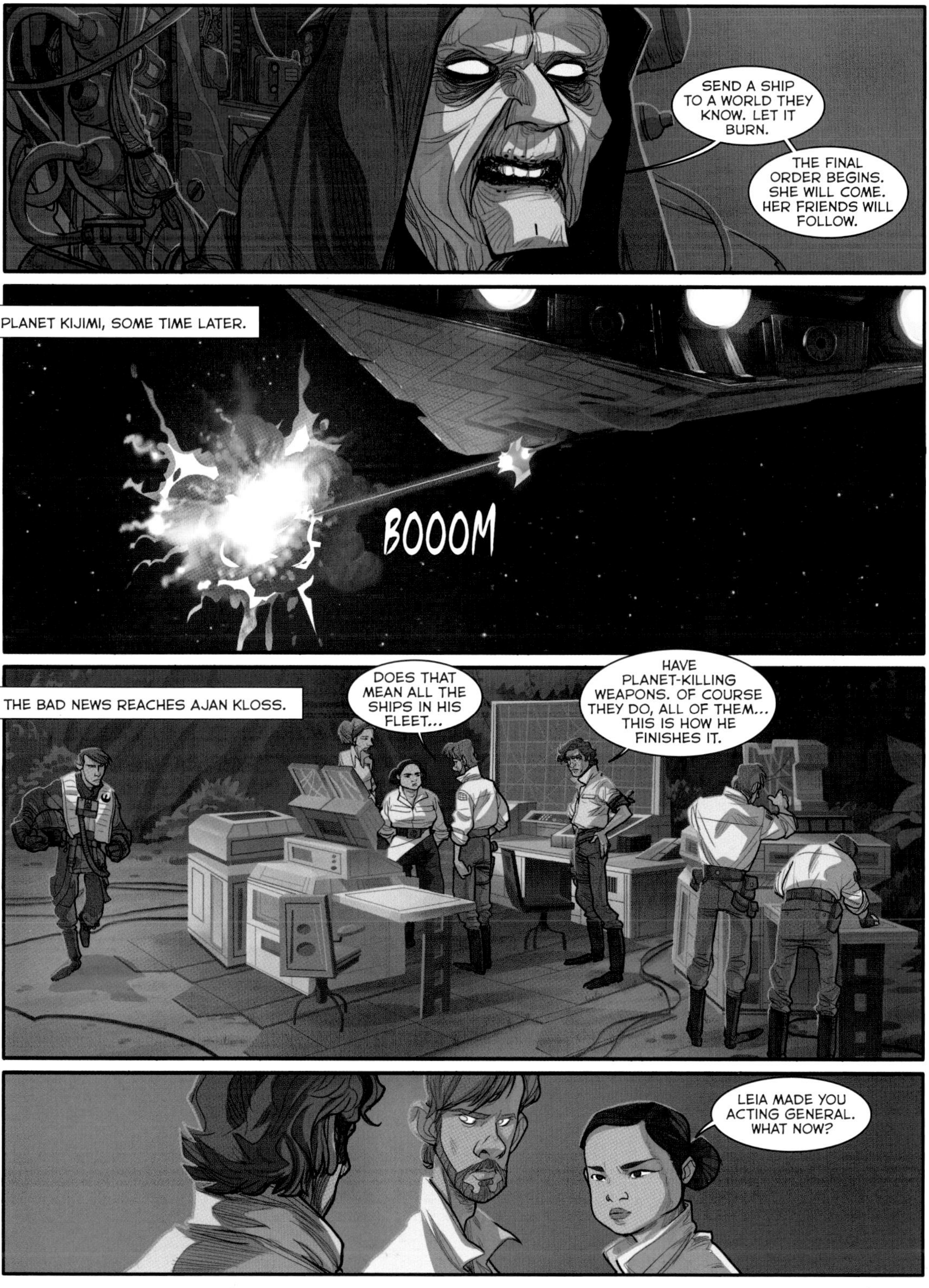
SEND A SHIP TO A WORLD THEY KNOW. LET IT BURN.
THE FINAL ORDER BEGINS. SHE WILL COME. HER FRIENDS WILL FOLLOW.
PLANET KIJIMI, SOME TIME LATER.
BOOOM
THE BAD NEWS REACHES AJAN KLOSS.
DOES THAT MEAN ALL THE SHIPS IN HIS FLEET...
HAVE PLANET-KILLING WEAPONS. OF COURSE THEY DO, ALL OF THEM... THIS IS HOW HE FINISHES IT.
LEIA MADE YOU ACTING GENERAL. WHAT NOW?

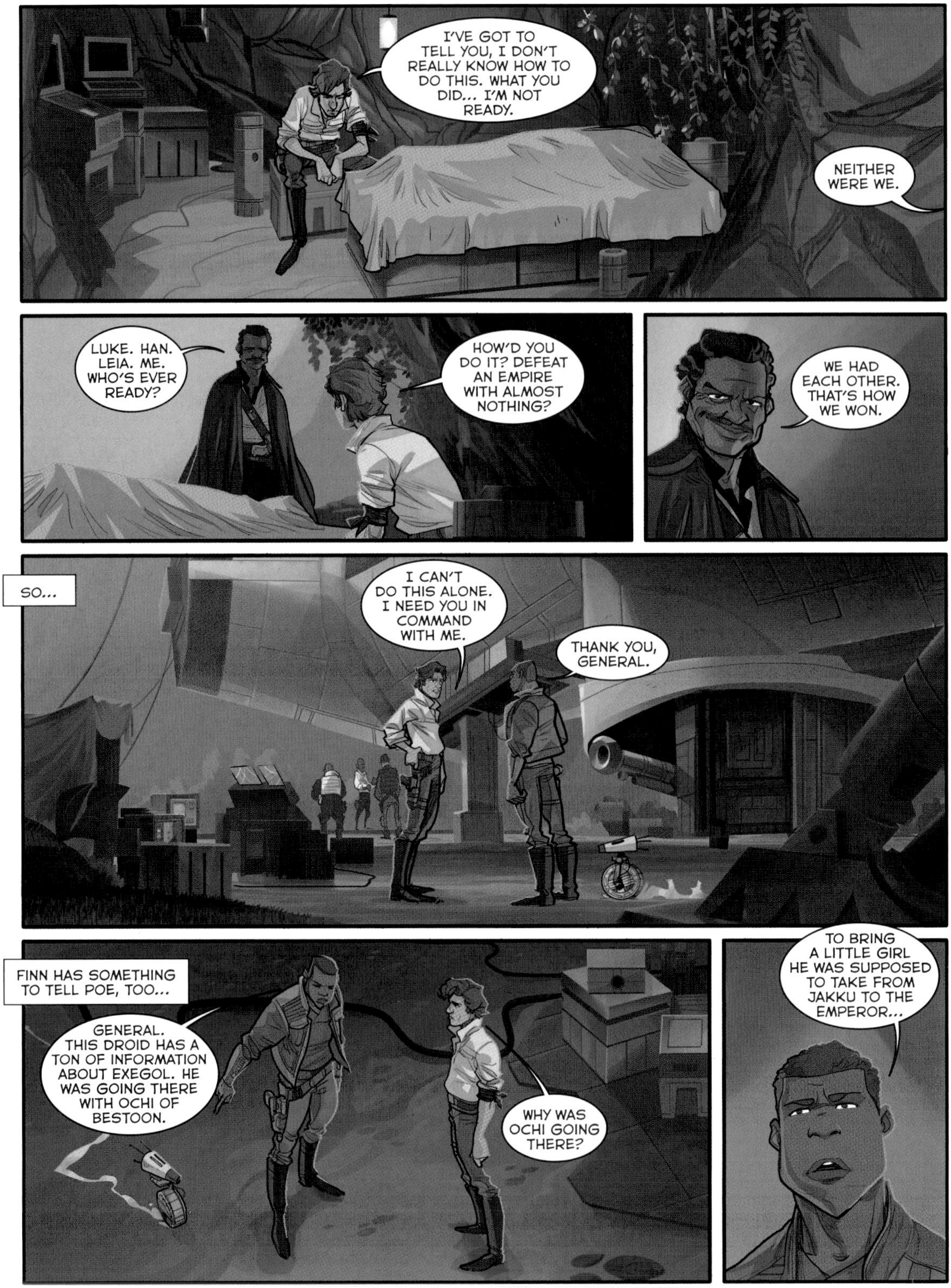
I'VE GOT TO TELL YOU, I DON'T REALLY KNOW HOW TO DO THIS. WHAT YOU DID... I'M NOT READY.
NEITHER WERE WE.
LUKE. HAN. LEIA. ME. WHO'S EVER READY?
HOW'D YOU DO IT? DEFEAT AN EMPIRE WITH ALMOST NOTHING?
WE HAD EACH OTHER. THAT'S HOW WE WON.
SO...
I CAN'T DO THIS ALONE. I NEED YOU IN COMMAND WITH ME.
THANK YOU, GENERAL.
FINN HAS SOMETHING TO TELL POE, TOO...
GENERAL. THIS DROID HAS A TON OF INFORMATION ABOUT EXEGOL. HE WAS GOING THERE WITH OCHI OF BESTOON.
WHY WAS OCHI GOING THERE?
TO BRING A LITTLE GIRL HE WAS SUPPOSED TO TAKE FROM JAKKU TO THE EMPEROR...

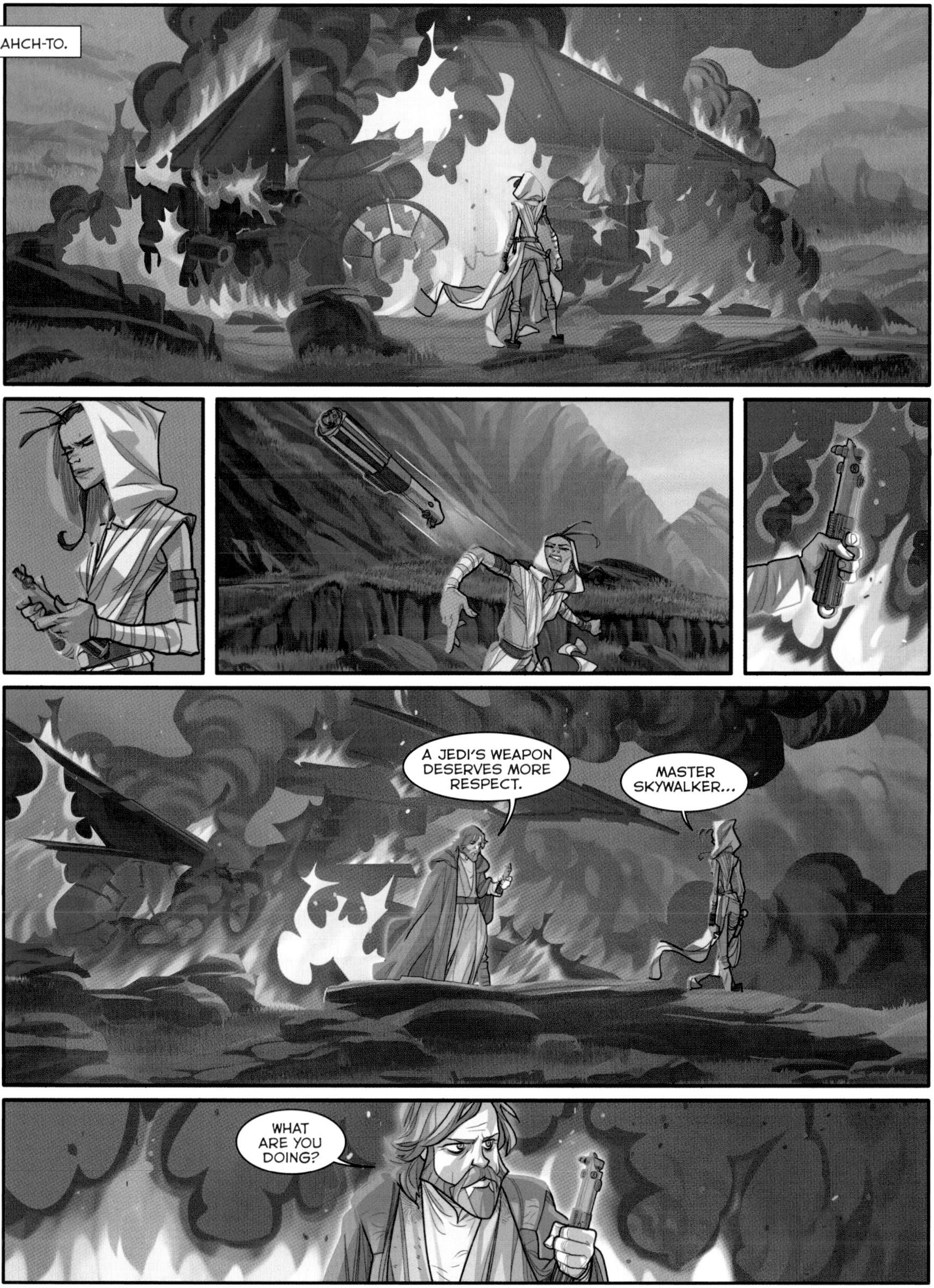
AHCH-TO.
A JEDI'S WEAPON DESERVES MORE RESPECT.
MASTER SKYWALKER...
WHAT ARE YOU DOING?

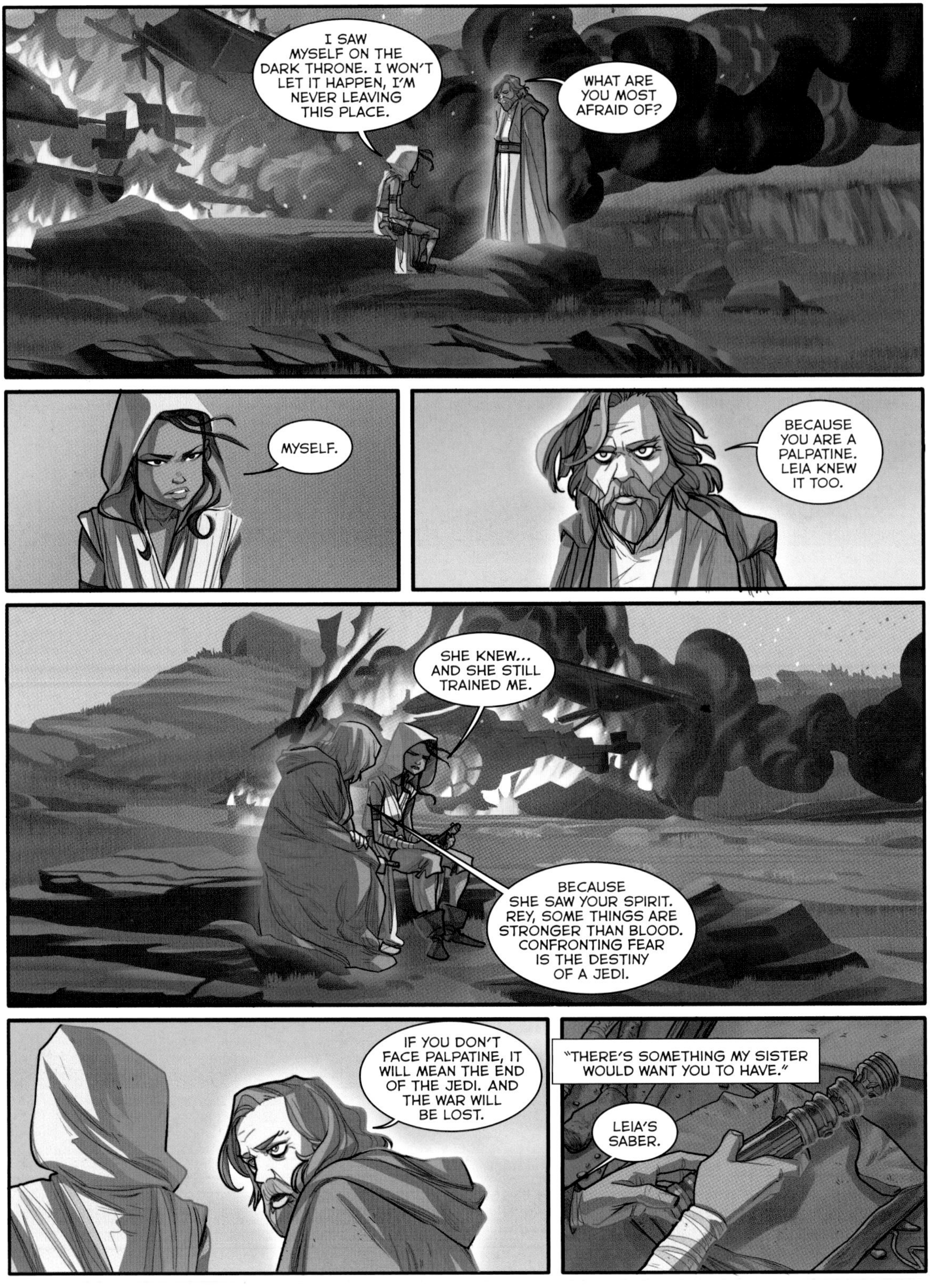
I SAW MYSELF ON THE DARK THRONE. I WON'T LET IT HAPPEN, I'M NEVER LEAVING THIS PLACE.
WHAT ARE YOU MOST AFRAID OF?
MYSELF.
BECAUSE YOU ARE A PALPATINE. LEIA KNEW IT TOO.
SHE KNEW... AND SHE STILL TRAINED ME.
BECAUSE SHE SAW YOUR SPIRIT. REY, SOME THINGS ARE STRONGER THAN BLOOD. CONFRONTING FEAR IS THE DESTINY OF A JEDI.
IF YOU DON'T FACE PALPATINE, IT WILL MEAN THE END OF THE JEDI. AND THE WAR WILL BE LOST.
"THERE'S SOMETHING MY SISTER WOULD WANT YOU TO HAVE."
LEIA'S SABER.

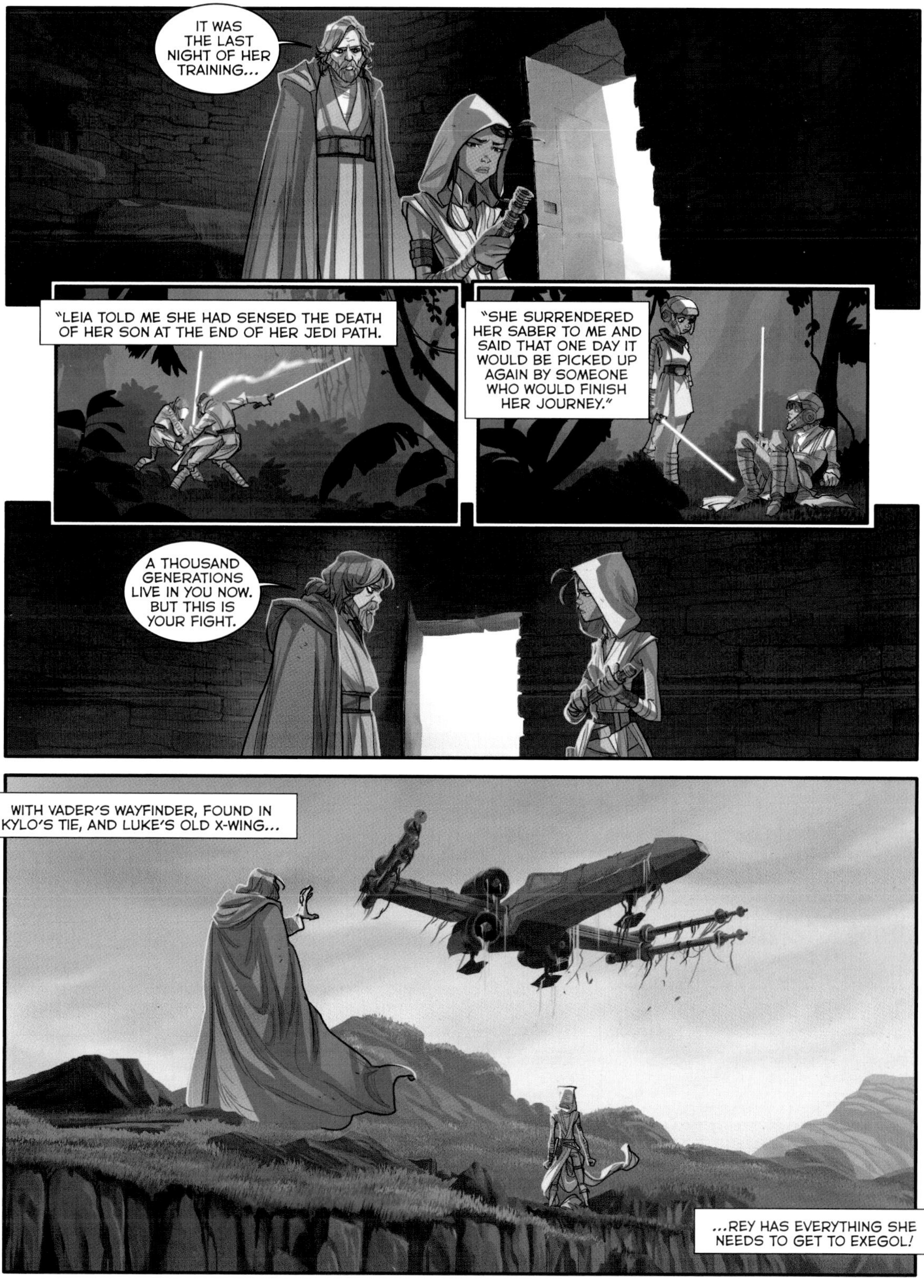
IT WAS THE LAST NIGHT OF HER TRAINING...
"LEIA TOLD ME SHE HAD SENSED THE DEATH OF HER SON AT THE END OF HER JEDI PATH.
"SHE SURRENDERED HER SABER TO ME AND SAID THAT ONE DAY IT WOULD BE PICKED UP AGAIN BY SOMEONE WHO WOULD FINISH HER JOURNEY."
A THOUSAND GENERATIONS LIVE IN YOU NOW. BUT THIS IS YOUR FIGHT.
WITH VADER'S WAYFINDER, FOUND IN KYLO'S TIE, AND LUKE'S OLD X-WING...
...REY HAS EVERYTHING SHE NEEDS TO GET TO EXEGOL!

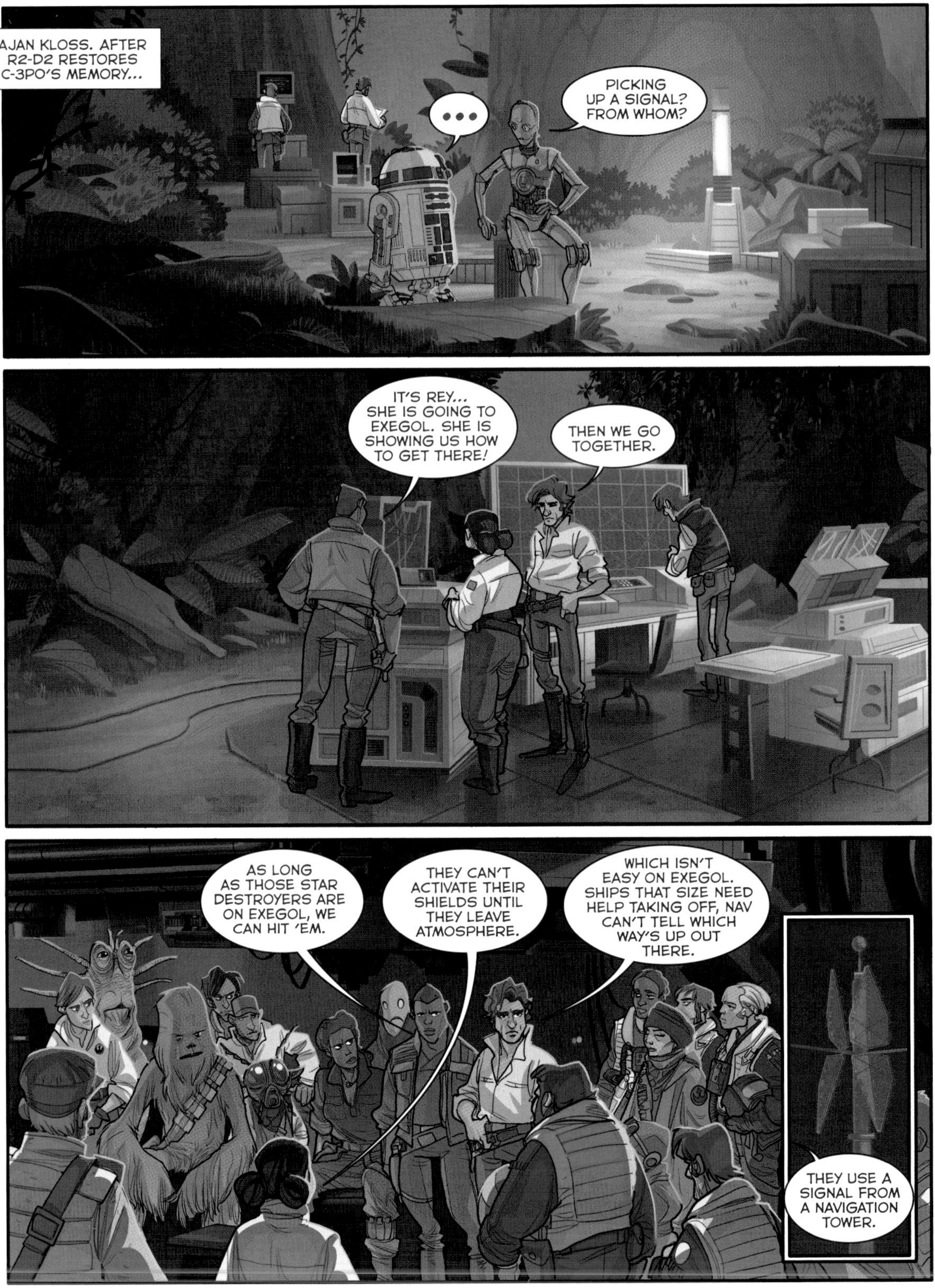
AJAN KLOSS. AFTER R2-D2 RESTORES C-3PO'S MEMORY...
•••
PICKING UP A SIGNAL? FROM WHOM?
IT'S REY... SHE IS GOING TO EXEGOL. SHE IS SHOWING US HOW TO GET THERE!
THEN WE GO TOGETHER.
AS LONG AS THOSE STAR DESTROYERS ARE ON EXEGOL, WE CAN HIT 'EM.
THEY CAN'T ACTIVATE THEIR SHIELDS UNTIL THEY LEAVE ATMOSPHERE.
WHICH ISN'T EASY ON EXEGOL. SHIPS THAT SIZE NEED HELP TAKING OFF, NAV CAN'T TELL WHICH WAY'S UP OUT THERE.
THEY USE A SIGNAL FROM A NAVIGATION TOWER.

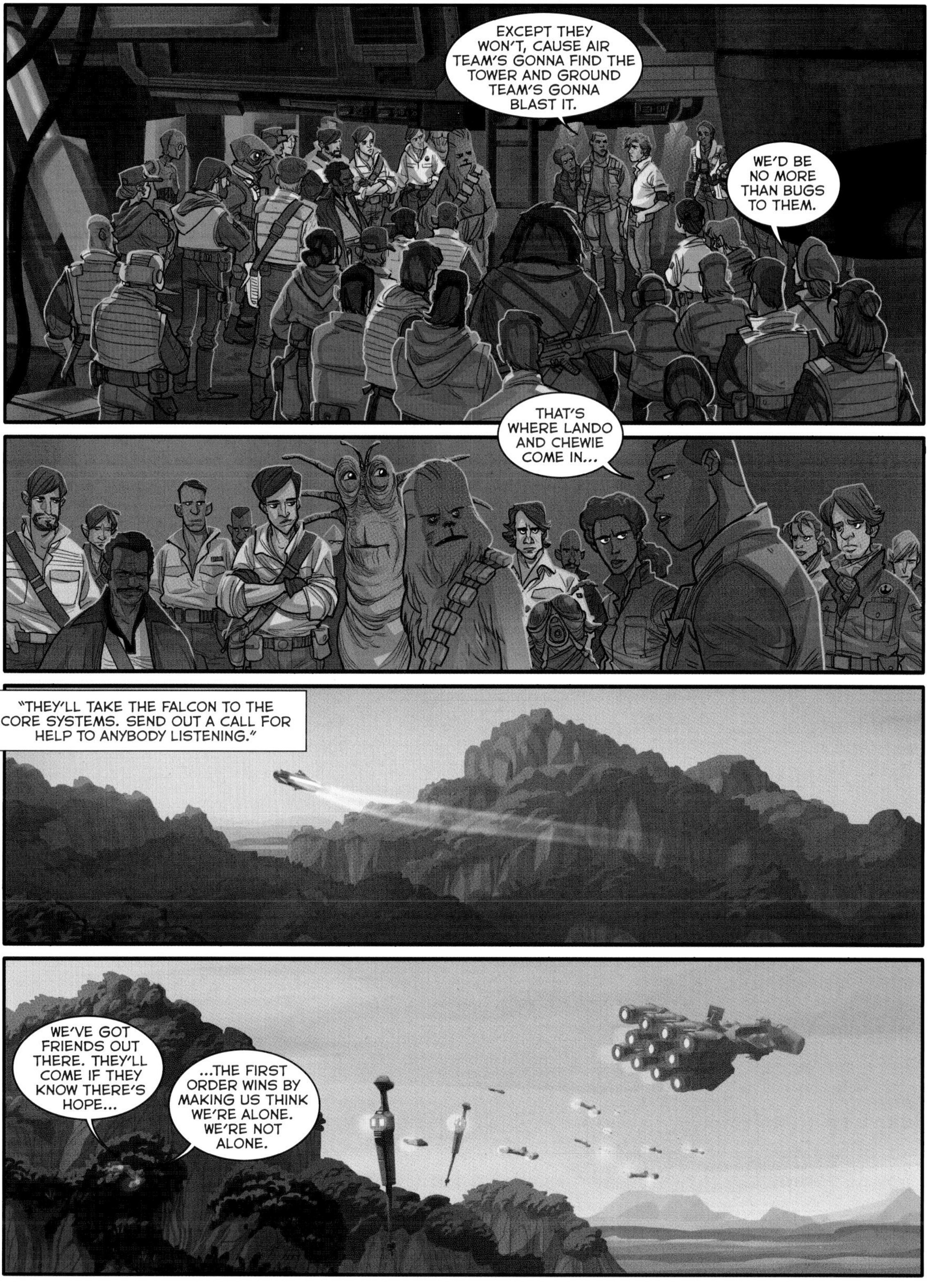
EXCEPT THEY WON'T, CAUSE AIR TEAM'S GONNA FIND THE TOWER AND GROUND TEAM'S GONNA BLAST IT.
WE'D BE NO MORE THAN BUGS TO THEM.
THAT'S WHERE LANDO AND CHEWIE COME IN...
"THEY'LL TAKE THE FALCON TO THE CORE SYSTEMS. SEND OUT A CALL FOR HELP TO ANYBODY LISTENING."
WE'VE GOT FRIENDS OUT THERE. THEY'LL COME IF THEY KNOW THERE'S HOPE...
...THE FIRST ORDER WINS BY MAKING US THINK WE'RE ALONE. WE'RE NOT ALONE.

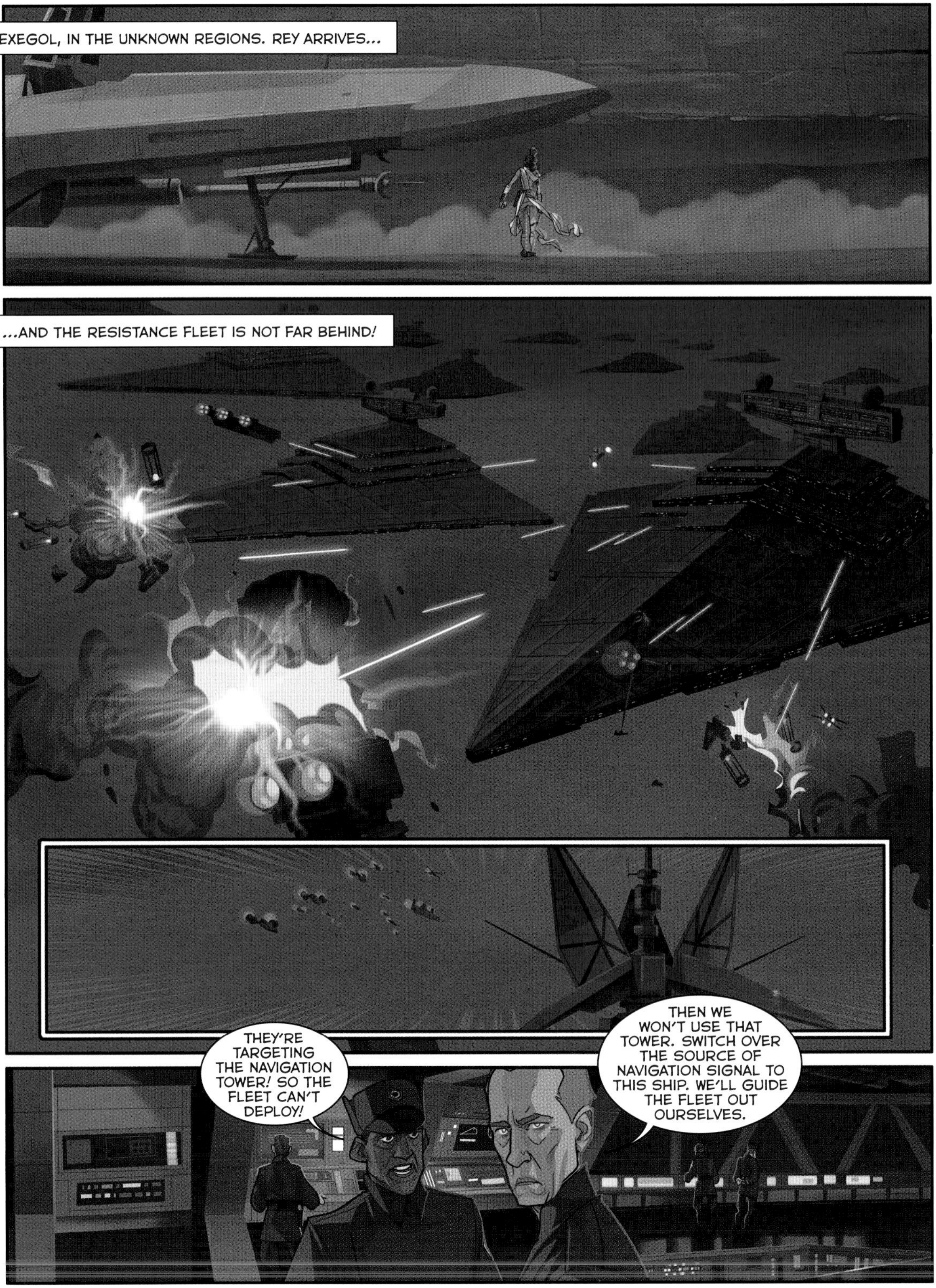
EXEGOL, IN THE UNKNOWN REGIONS. REY ARRIVES...
...AND THE RESISTANCE FLEET IS NOT FAR BEHIND!
THEY'RE TARGETING THE NAVIGATION TOWER! SO THE FLEET CAN'T DEPLOY!
THEN WE WON'T USE THAT TOWER. SWITCH OVER THE SOURCE OF NAVIGATION SIGNAL TO THIS SHIP. WE'LL GUIDE THE FLEET OUT OURSELVES.

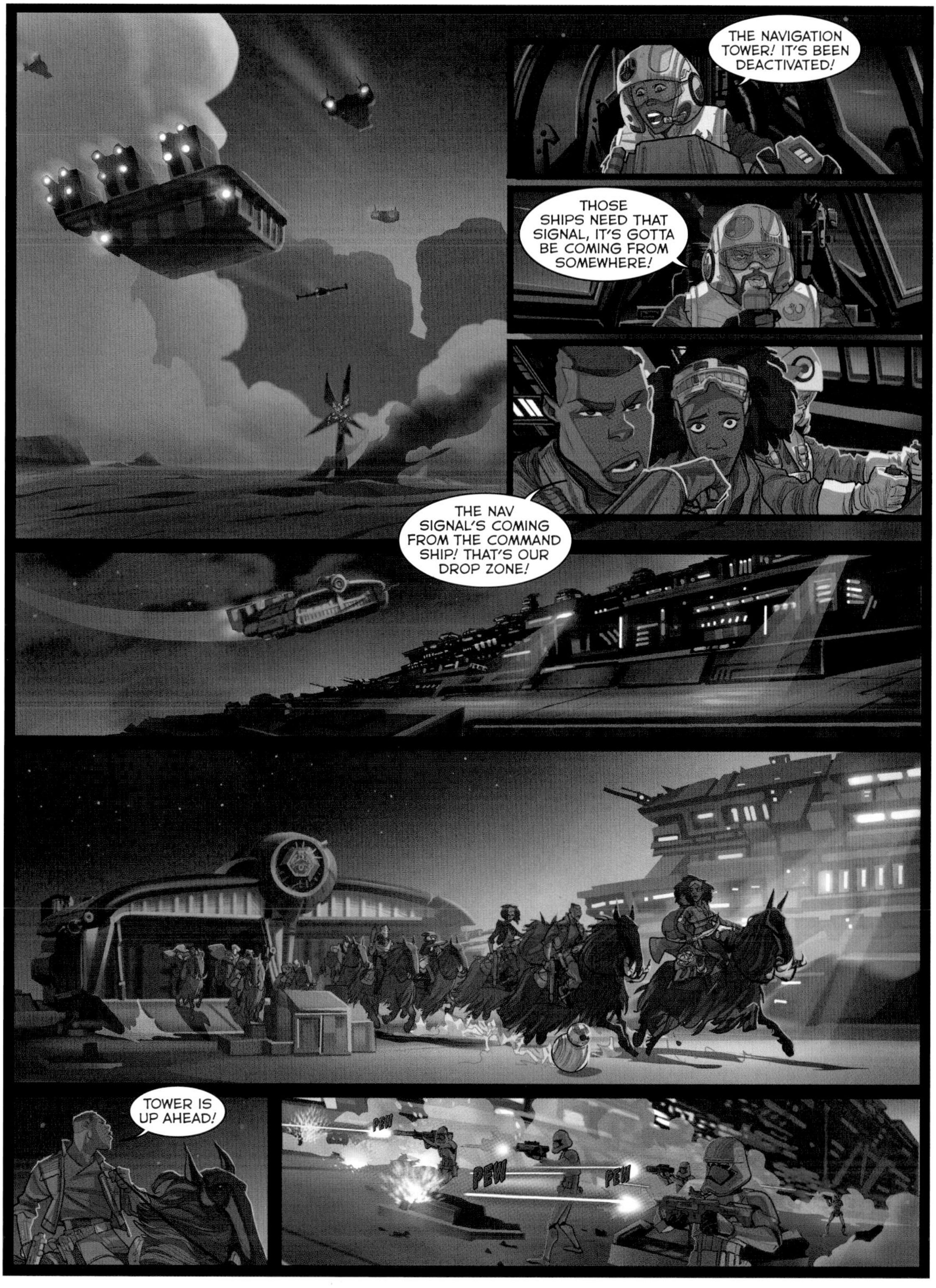
THE NAVIGATION TOWER! IT'S BEEN DEACTIVATED!
THOSE SHIPS NEED THAT SIGNAL, IT'S GOTTA BE COMING FROM SOMEWHERE!
THE NAV SIGNAL'S COMING FROM THE COMMAND SHIP! THAT'S OUR DROP ZONE!
TOWER IS UP AHEAD!
PEW
PEW
PEW

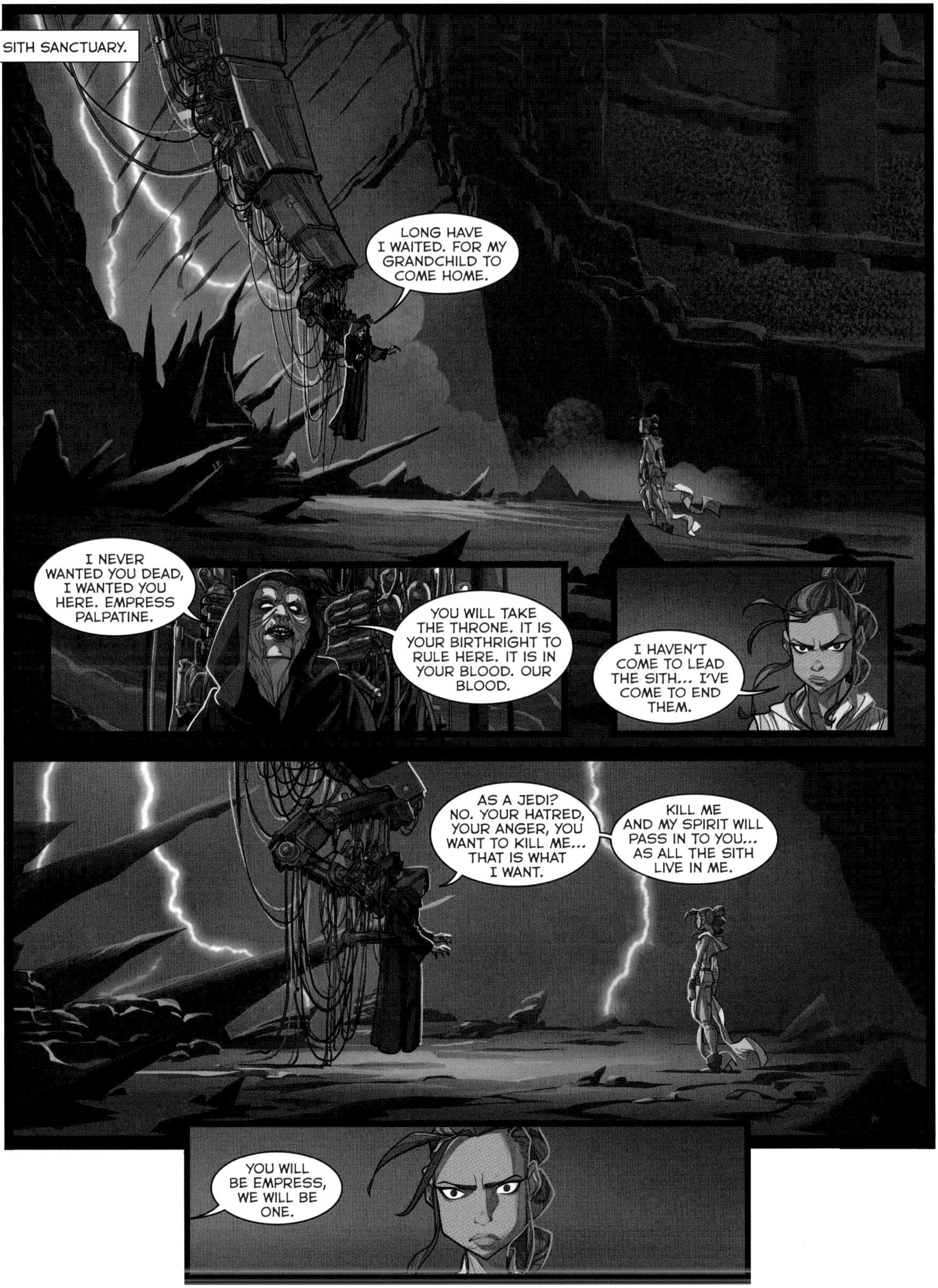
SITH SANCTUARY.
LONG HAVE I WAITED. FOR MY GRANDCHILD TO COME HOME.
I NEVER WANTED YOU DEAD, I WANTED YOU HERE. EMPRESS PALPATINE.
YOU WILL TAKE THE THRONE. IT IS YOUR BIRTHRIGHT TO RULE HERE. IT IS IN YOUR BLOOD. OUR BLOOD.
I HAVEN'T COME TO LEAD THE SITH... I'VE COME TO END THEM.
AS A JEDI? NO. YOUR HATRED, YOUR ANGER, YOU WANT TO KILL ME... THAT IS WHAT I WANT.
KILL ME AND MY SPIRIT WILL PASS IN TO YOU... AS ALL THE SITH LIVE IN ME.
YOU WILL BE EMPRESS, WE WILL BE ONE.

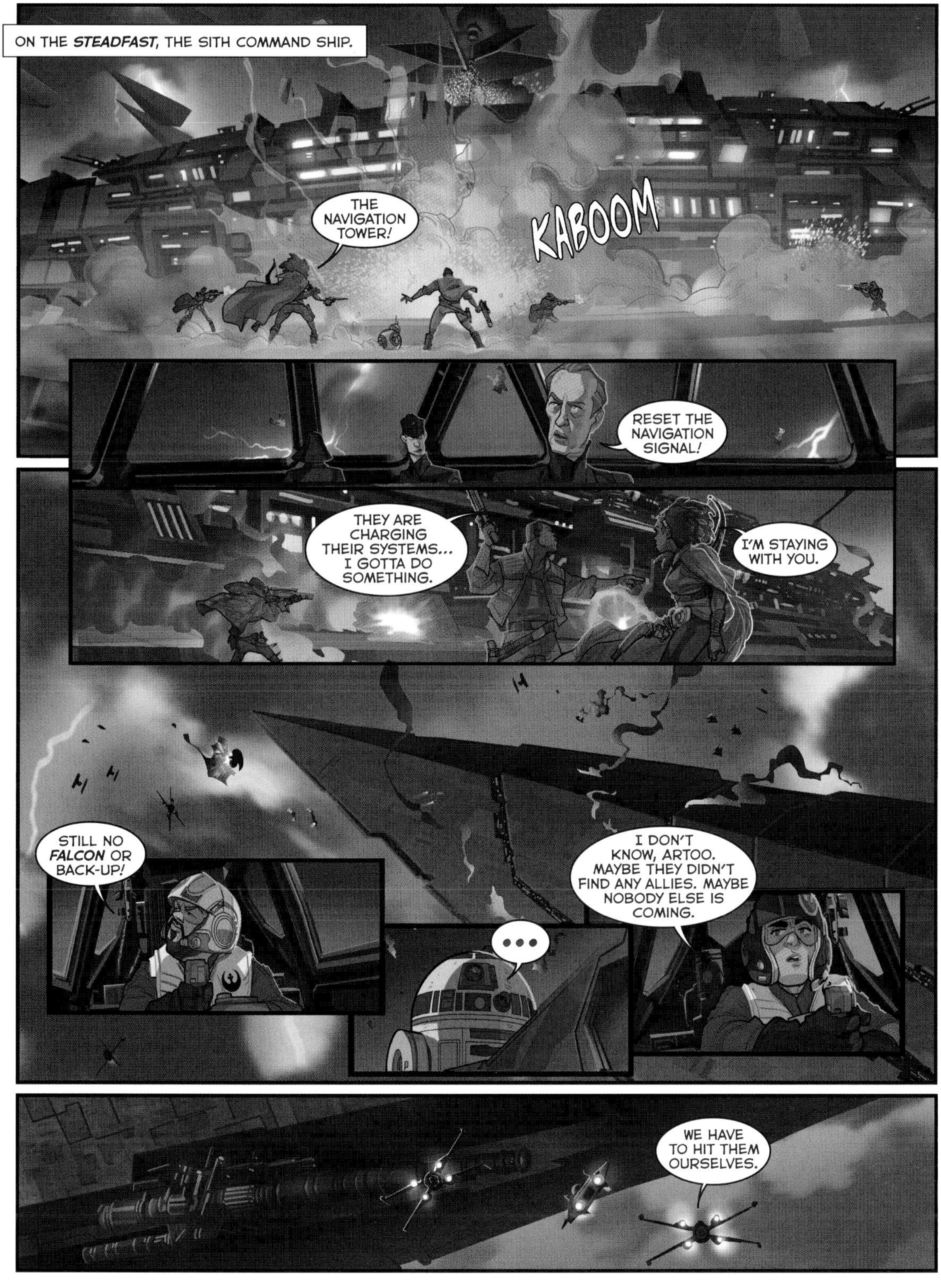
ON THE *STEADFAST*, THE SITH COMMAND SHIP.
THE NAVIGATION TOWER!
KABOOM
RESET THE NAVIGATION SIGNAL!
THEY ARE CHARGING THEIR SYSTEMS... I GOTTA DO SOMETHING.
I'M STAYING WITH YOU.
STILL NO *FALCON* OR BACK-UP!
...
I DON'T KNOW, ARTOO. MAYBE THEY DIDN'T FIND ANY ALLIES. MAYBE NOBODY ELSE IS COMING.
WE HAVE TO HIT THEM OURSELVES.

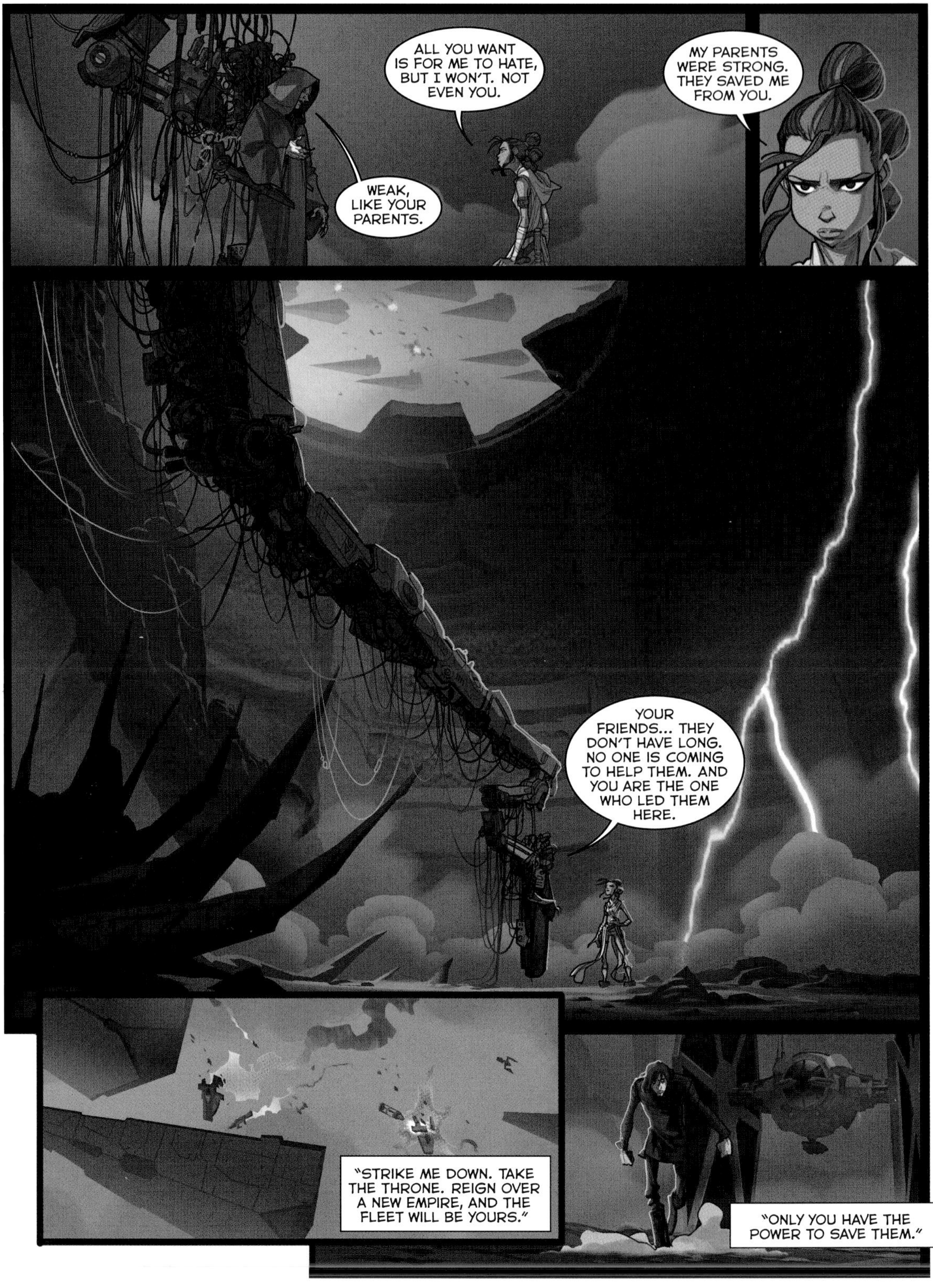
ALL YOU WANT IS FOR ME TO HATE, BUT I WON'T. NOT EVEN YOU.
WEAK, LIKE YOUR PARENTS.
MY PARENTS WERE STRONG. THEY SAVED ME FROM YOU.
YOUR FRIENDS... THEY DON'T HAVE LONG. NO ONE IS COMING TO HELP THEM. AND YOU ARE THE ONE WHO LED THEM HERE.
"STRIKE ME DOWN. TAKE THE THRONE. REIGN OVER A NEW EMPIRE, AND THE FLEET WILL BE YOURS."
"ONLY YOU HAVE THE POWER TO SAVE THEM."

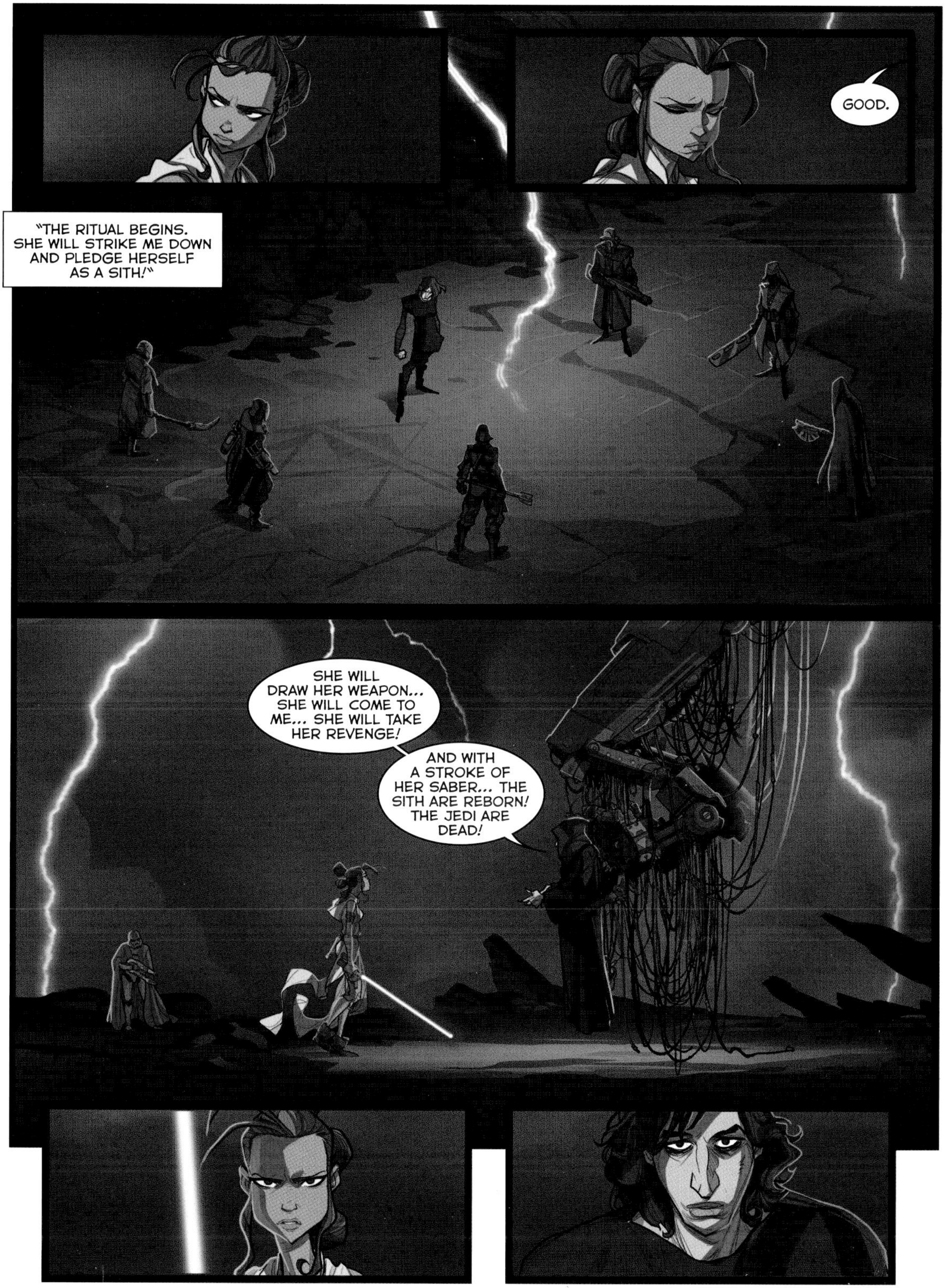
GOOD.
"THE RITUAL BEGINS. SHE WILL STRIKE ME DOWN AND PLEDGE HERSELF AS A SITH!"
SHE WILL DRAW HER WEAPON... SHE WILL COME TO ME... SHE WILL TAKE HER REVENGE!
AND WITH A STROKE OF HER SABER... THE SITH ARE REBORN! THE JEDI ARE DEAD!

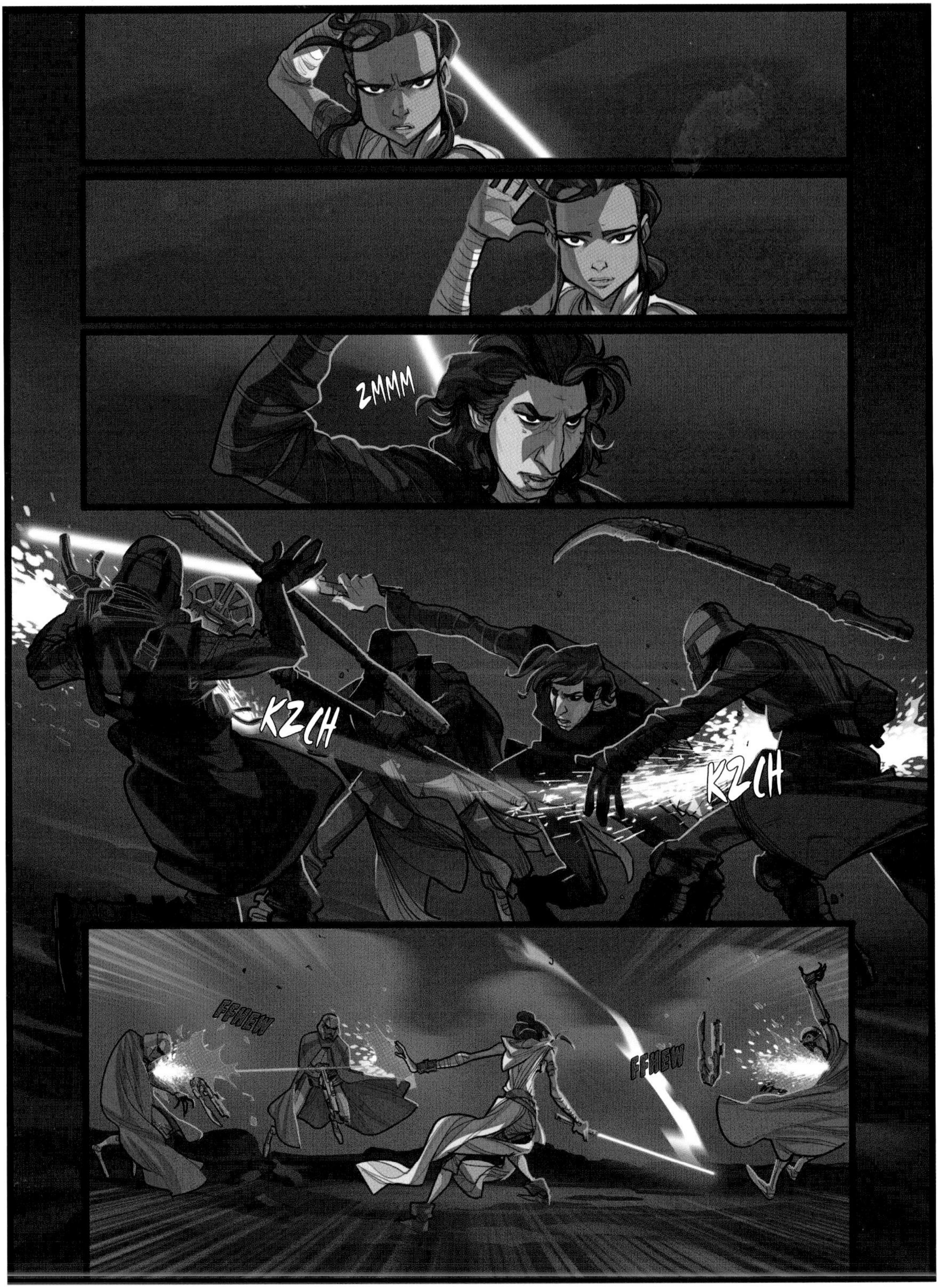
ZMMM
KZCH
KZCH
FFHEW
FFHEW

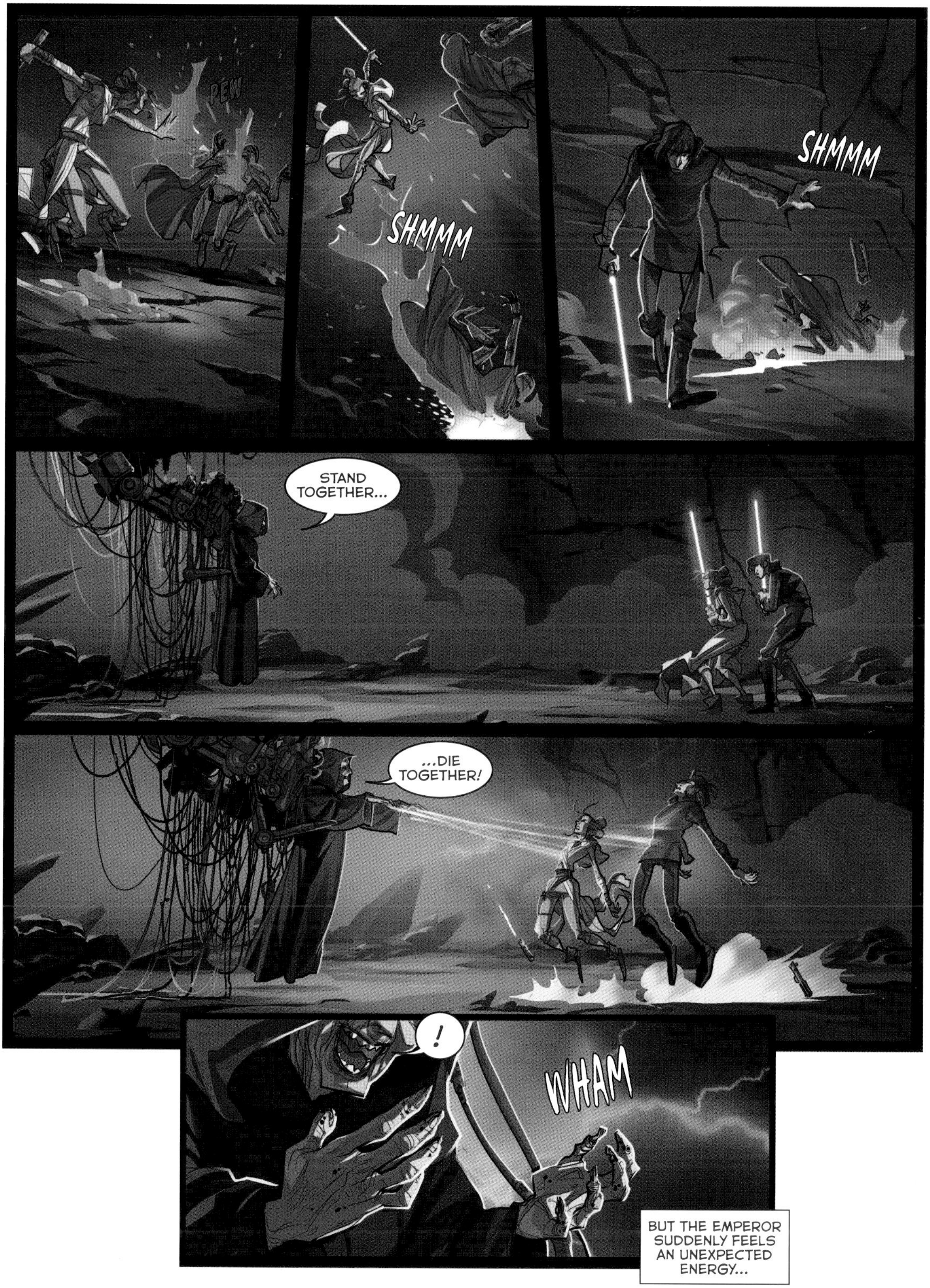
PEW
SHMMM
SHMMM
STAND TOGETHER...
...DIE TOGETHER!
!
WHAM
BUT THE EMPEROR SUDDENLY FEELS AN UNEXPECTED ENERGY...

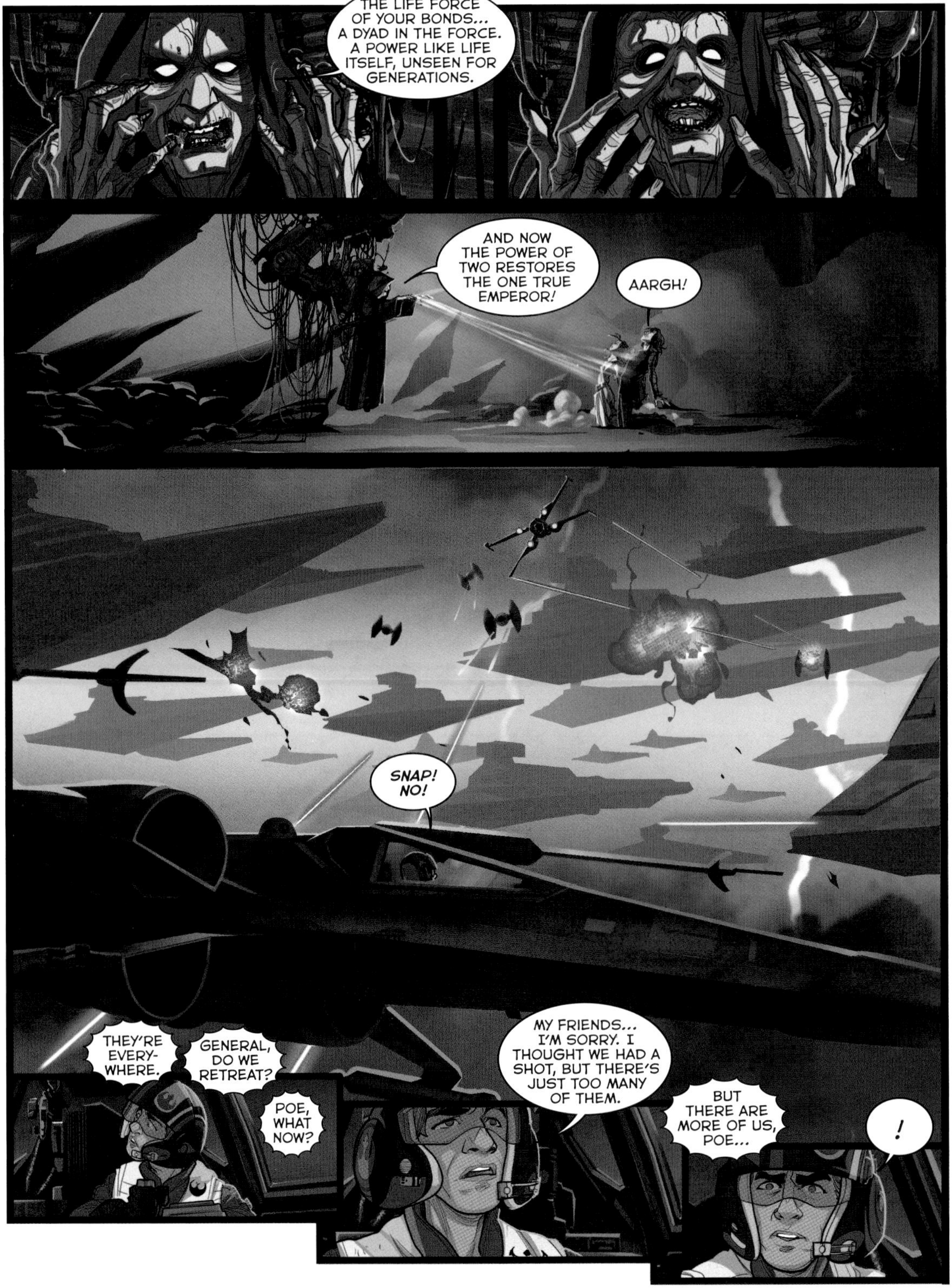
THE LIFE FORCE OF YOUR BONDS... A DYAD IN THE FORCE. A POWER LIKE LIFE ITSELF, UNSEEN FOR GENERATIONS.
AND NOW THE POWER OF TWO RESTORES THE ONE TRUE EMPEROR!
AARGH!
SNAP! NO!
THEY'RE EVERY-WHERE.
GENERAL, DO WE RETREAT?
POE, WHAT NOW?
MY FRIENDS... I'M SORRY. I THOUGHT WE HAD A SHOT, BUT THERE'S JUST TOO MANY OF THEM.
BUT THERE ARE MORE OF US, POE...
!

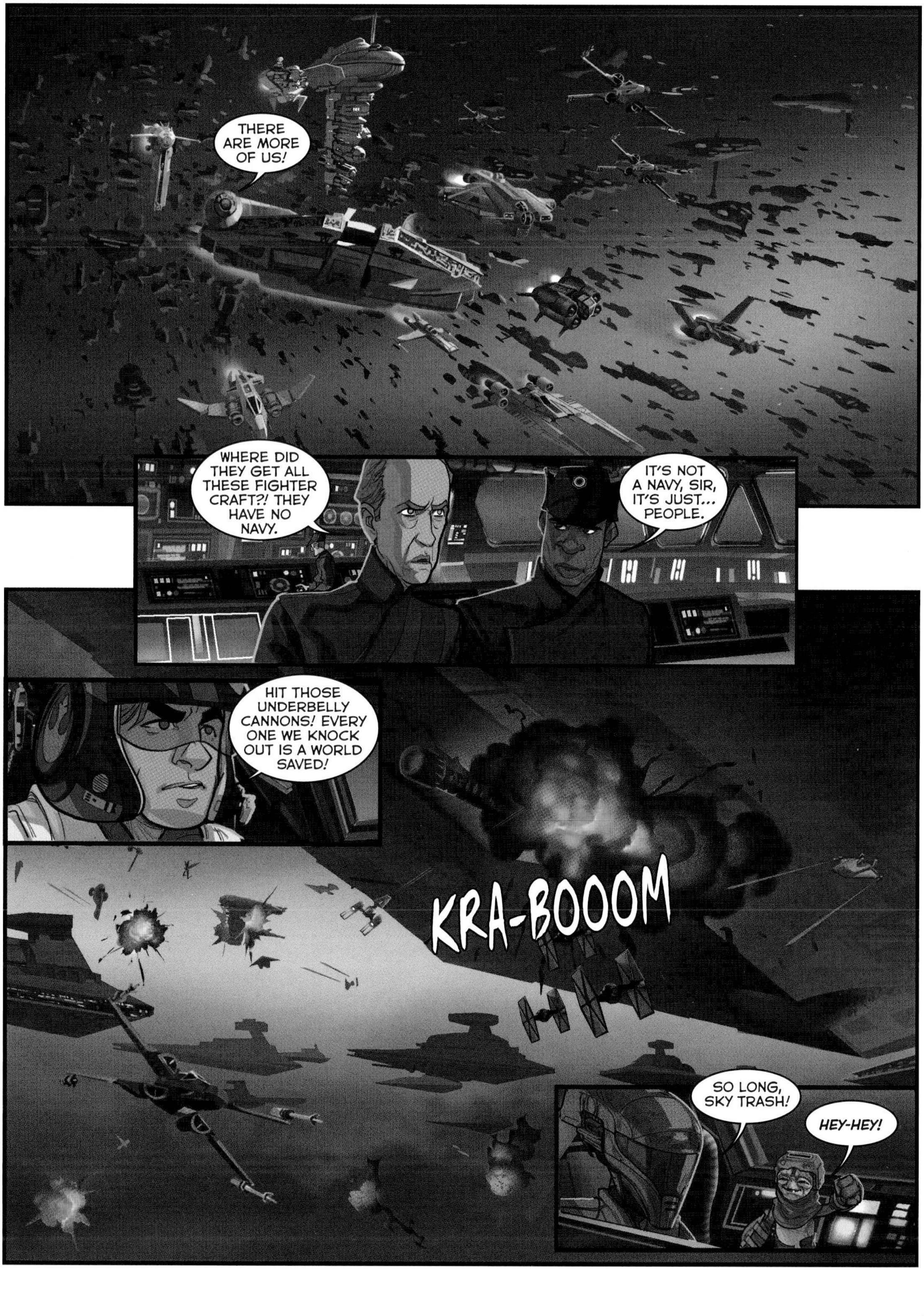

THERE ARE MORE OF US!
WHERE DID THEY GET ALL THESE FIGHTER CRAFT?! THEY HAVE NO NAVY.
IT'S NOT A NAVY, SIR, IT'S JUST... PEOPLE.
HIT THOSE UNDERBELLY CANNONS! EVERY ONE WE KNOCK OUT IS A WORLD SAVED!
KRA-BOOOM
SO LONG, SKY TRASH!
HEY-HEY!

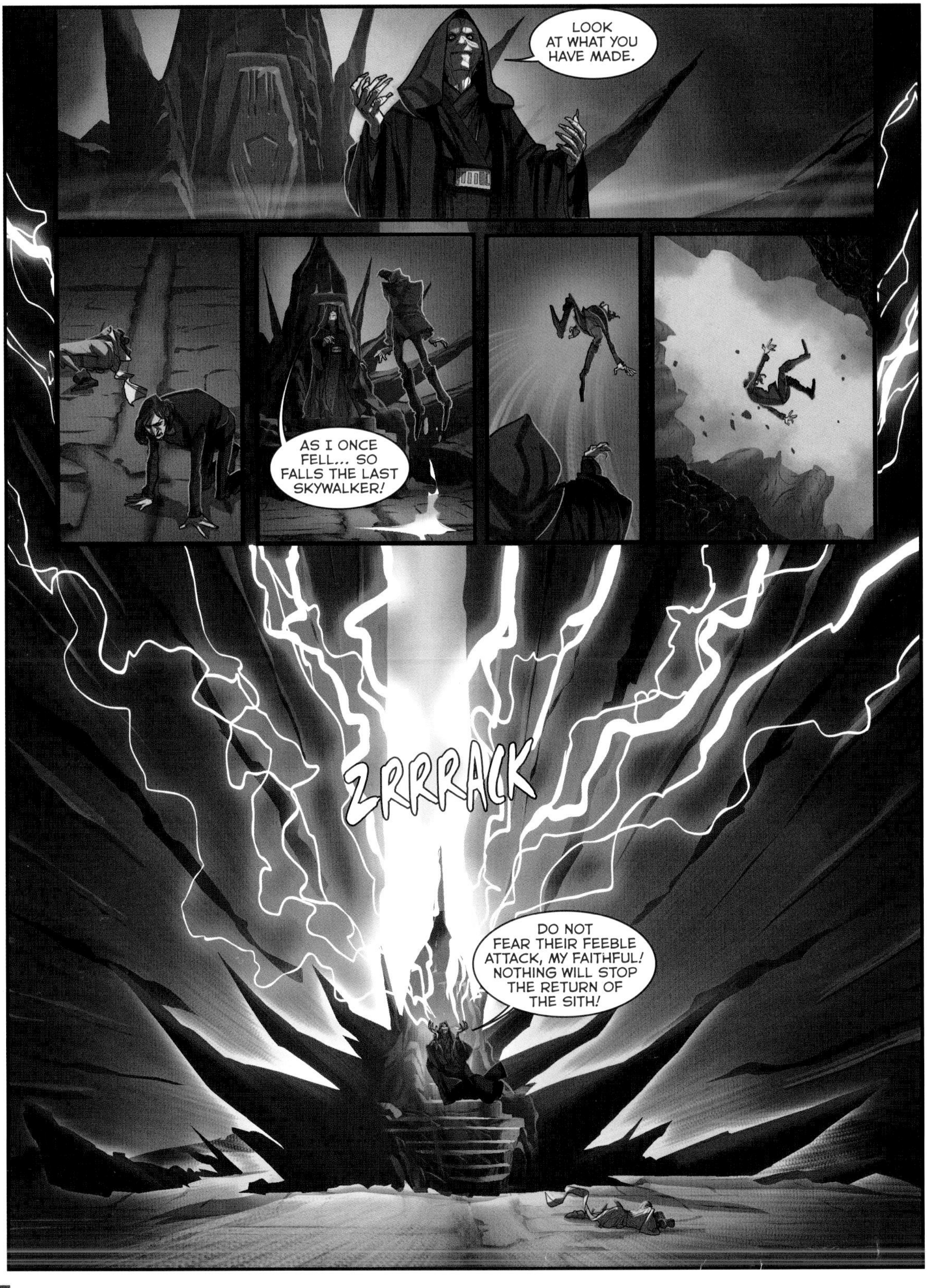
LOOK AT WHAT YOU HAVE MADE.
AS I ONCE FELL... SO FALLS THE LAST SKYWALKER!
ZRRRACK
DO NOT FEAR THEIR FEEBLE ATTACK, MY FAITHFUL! NOTHING WILL STOP THE RETURN OF THE SITH!

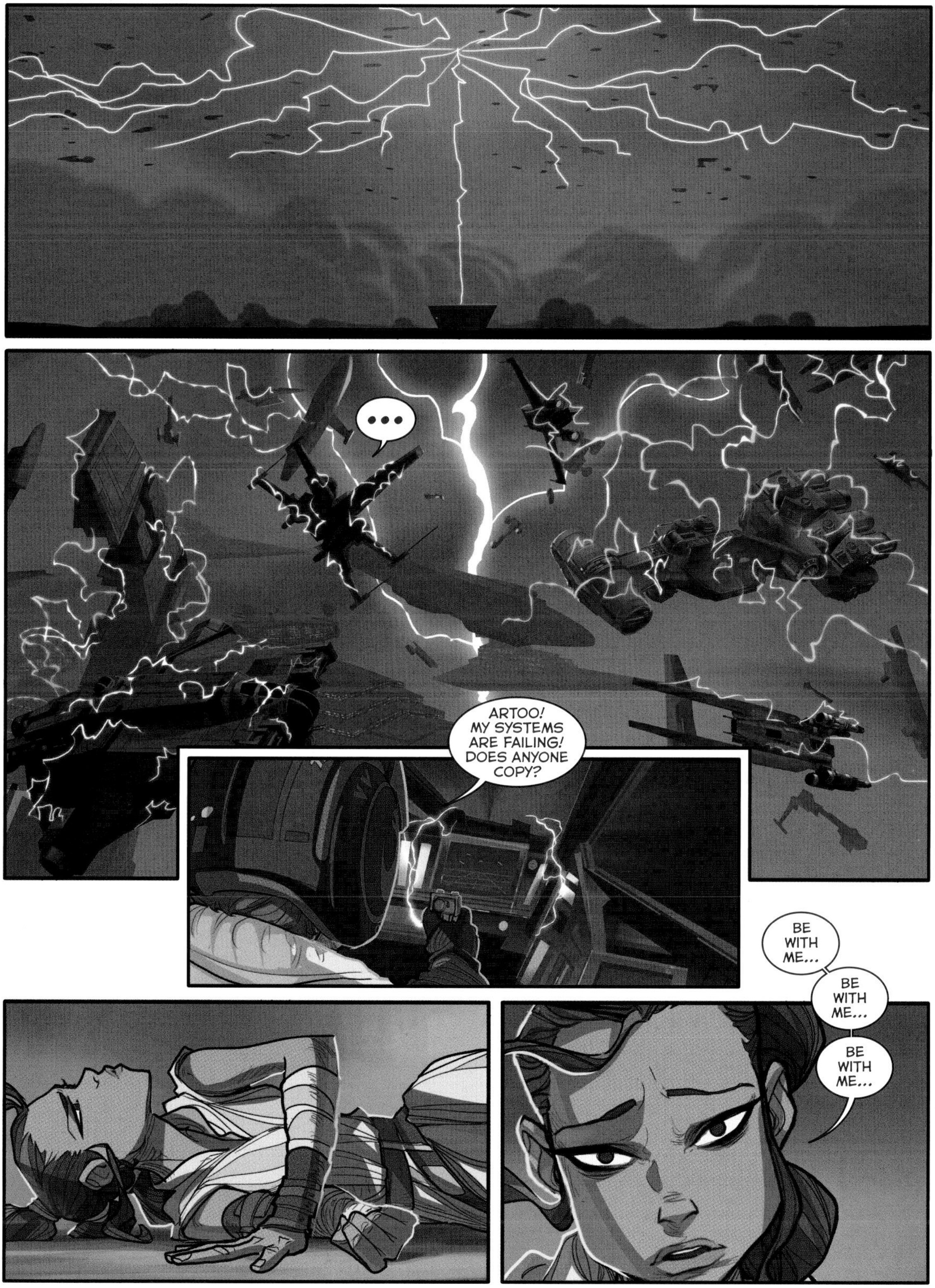
...
ARTOO! MY SYSTEMS ARE FAILING! DOES ANYONE COPY?
BE WITH ME...
BE WITH ME...
BE WITH ME...

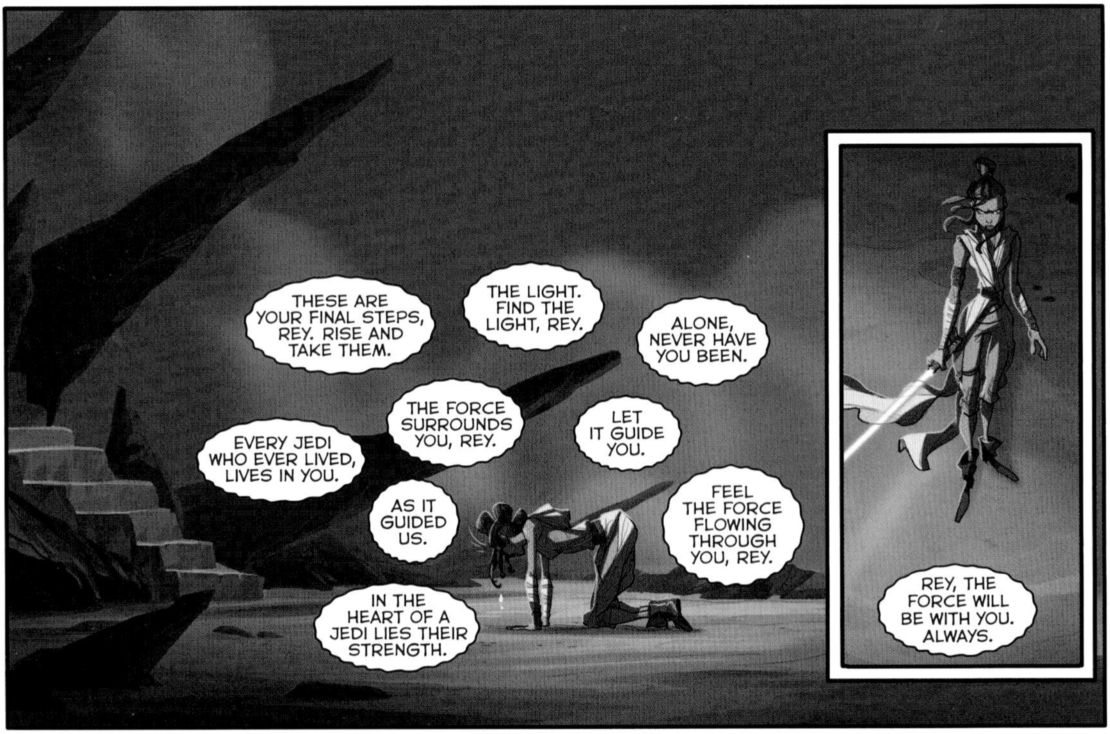
THESE ARE YOUR FINAL STEPS, REY. RISE AND TAKE THEM.
THE LIGHT. FIND THE LIGHT, REY.
ALONE, NEVER HAVE YOU BEEN.
THE FORCE SURROUNDS YOU, REY.
LET IT GUIDE YOU.
EVERY JEDI WHO EVER LIVED, LIVES IN YOU.
AS IT GUIDED US.
FEEL THE FORCE FLOWING THROUGH YOU, REY.
IN THE HEART OF A JEDI LIES THEIR STRENGTH.
REY, THE FORCE WILL BE WITH YOU. ALWAYS.

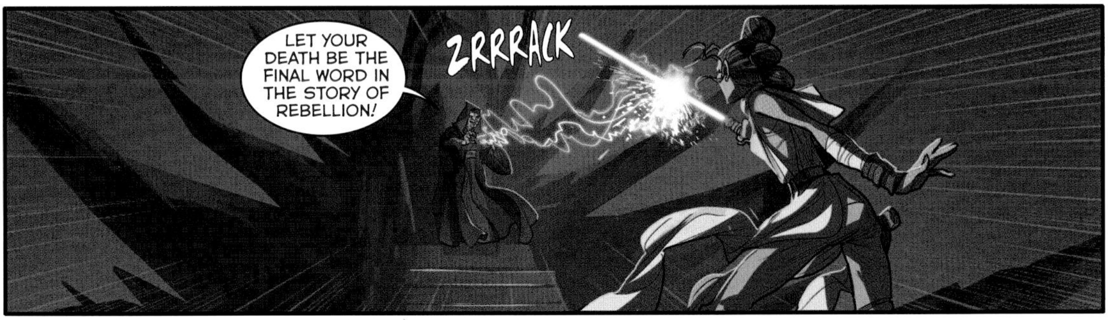
LET YOUR DEATH BE THE FINAL WORD IN THE STORY OF REBELLION!
ZRRRACK

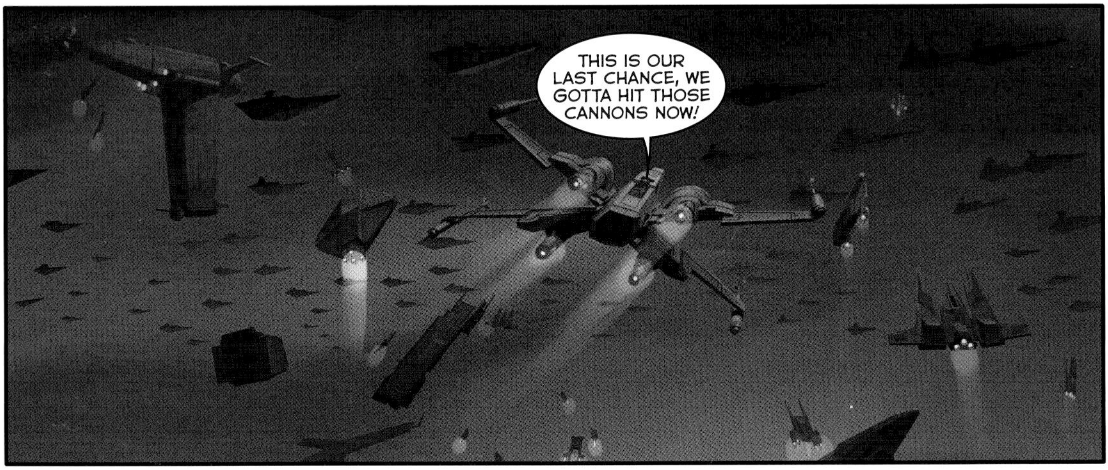
THIS IS OUR LAST CHANCE, WE GOTTA HIT THOSE CANNONS NOW!

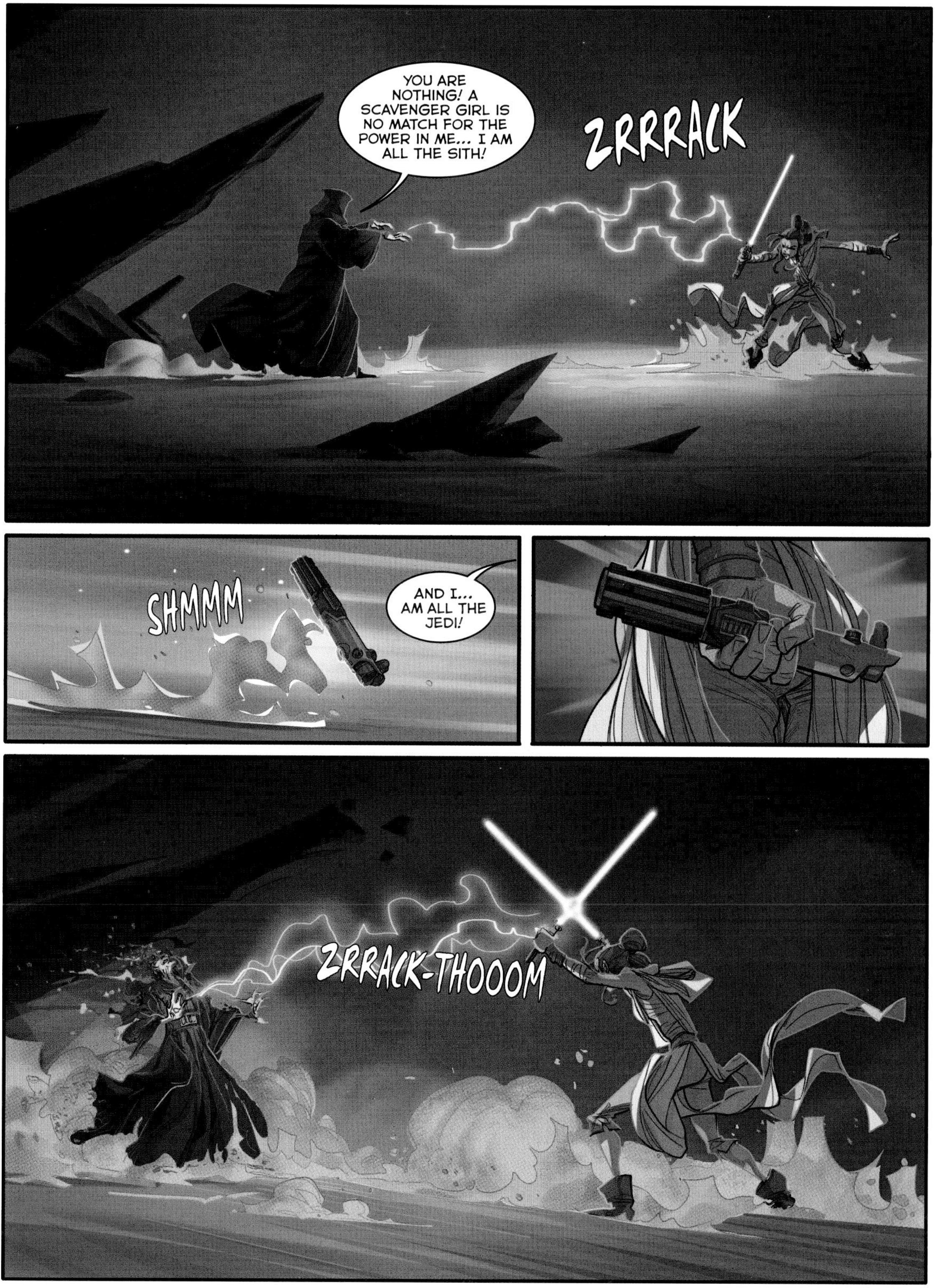
YOU ARE NOTHING! A SCAVENGER GIRL IS NO MATCH FOR THE POWER IN ME... I AM ALL THE SITH!
ZRRRACK
SHMMM
AND I... AM ALL THE JEDI!
ZRRACK-THOOOM

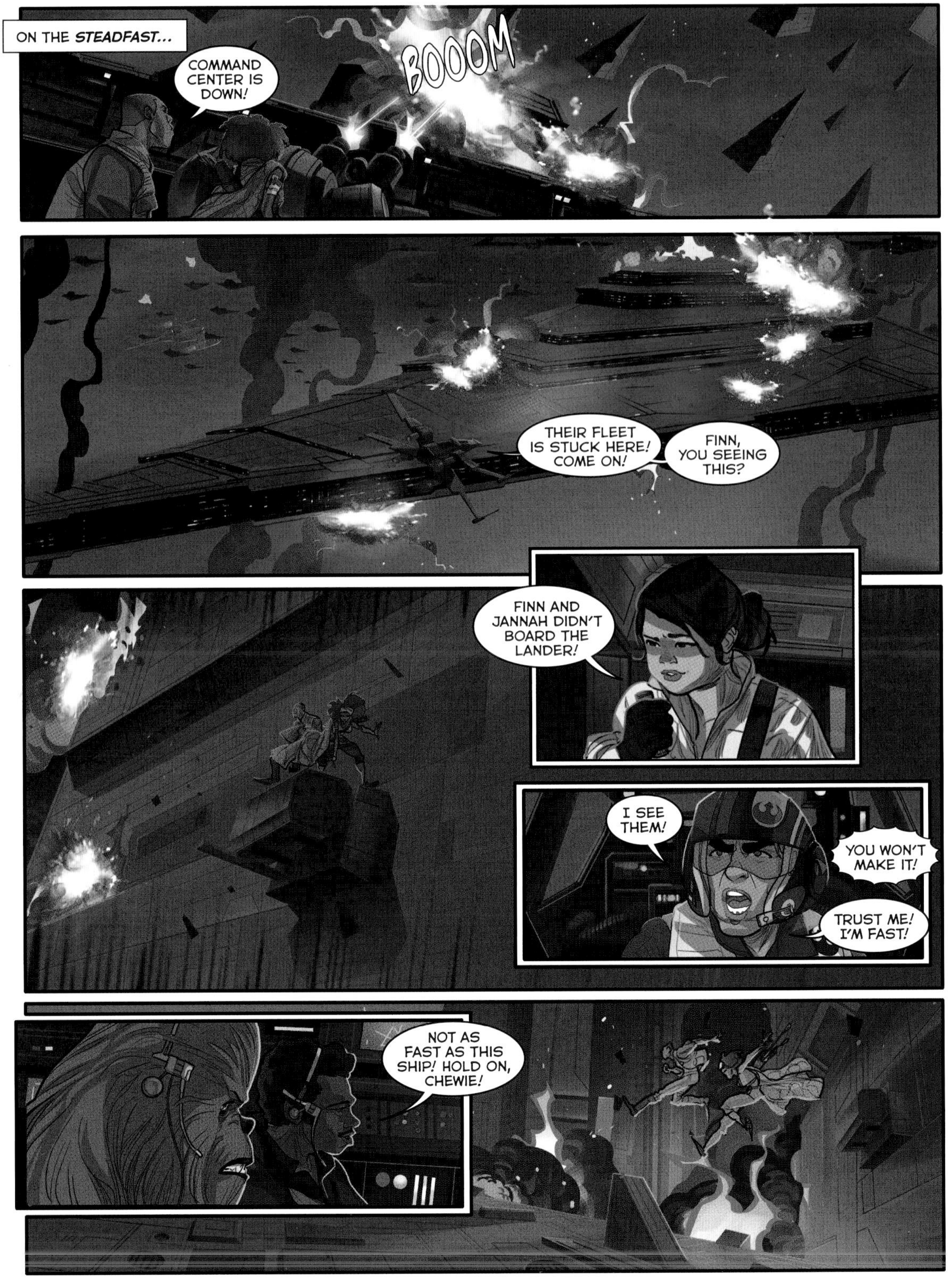
ON THE STEADFAST...
COMMAND CENTER IS DOWN!
BOOOM
THEIR FLEET IS STUCK HERE! COME ON!
FINN, YOU SEEING THIS?
FINN AND JANNAH DIDN'T BOARD THE LANDER!
I SEE THEM!
YOU WON'T MAKE IT!
TRUST ME! I'M FAST!
NOT AS FAST AS THIS SHIP! HOLD ON, CHEWIE!

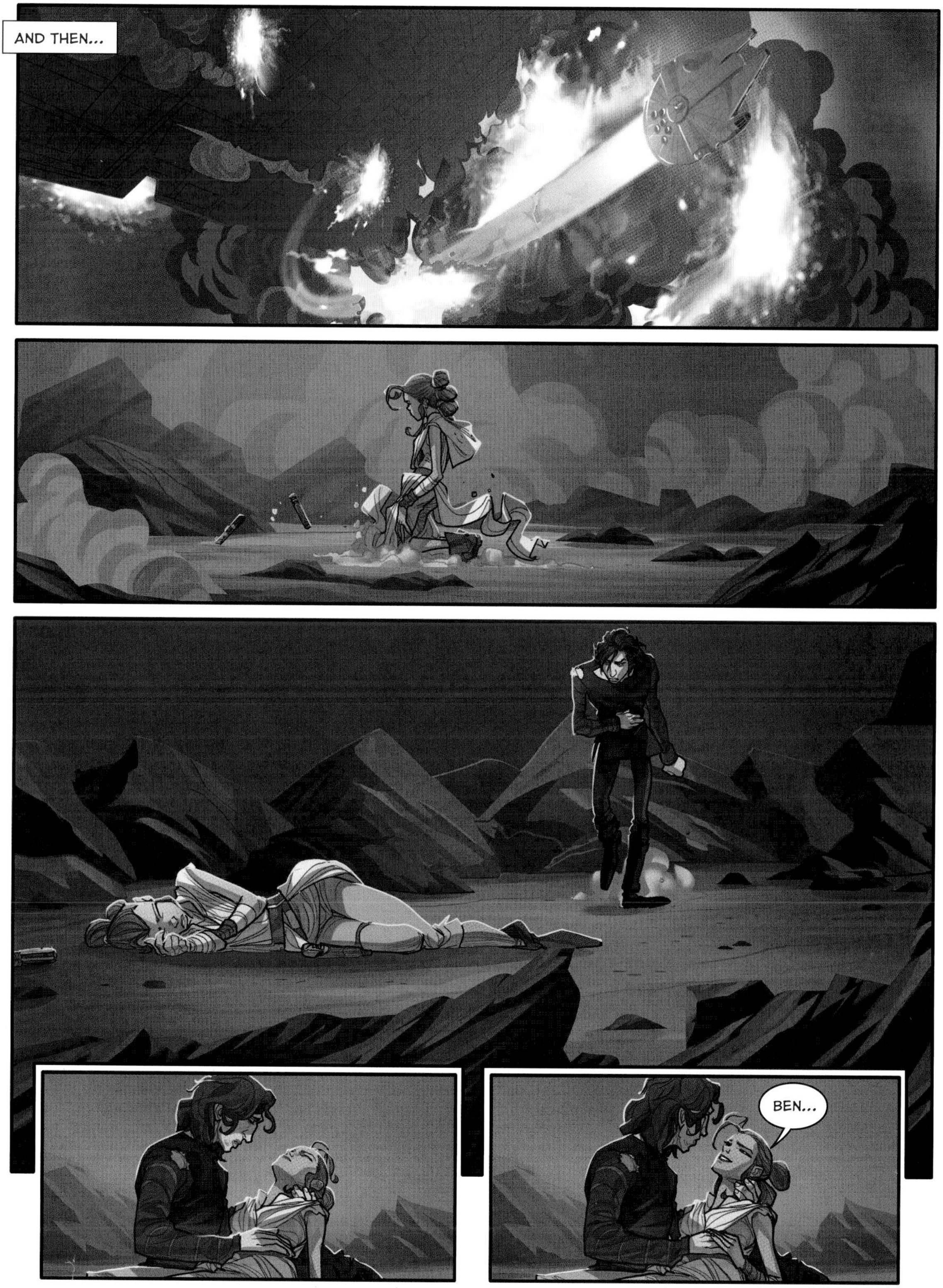
AND THEN...
BEN...

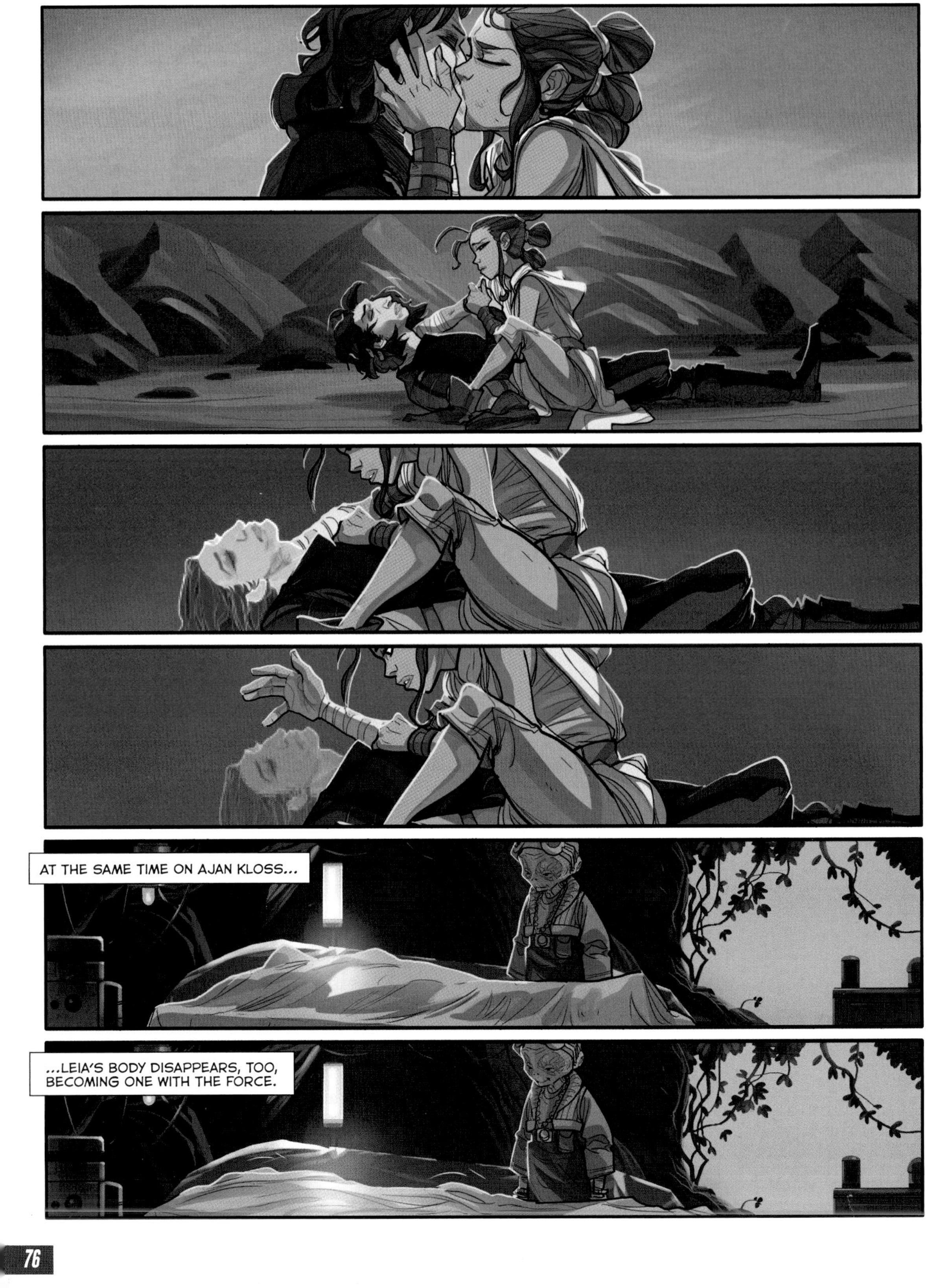
AT THE SAME TIME ON AJAN KLOSS...
...LEIA'S BODY DISAPPEARS, TOO, BECOMING ONE WITH THE FORCE.

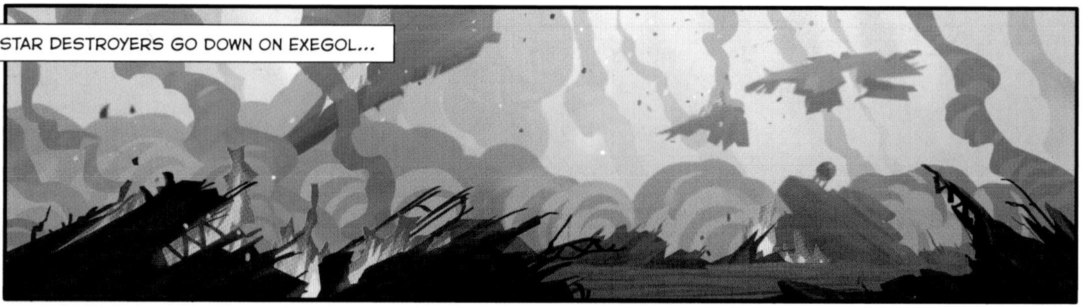
STAR DESTROYERS GO DOWN ON EXEGOL...

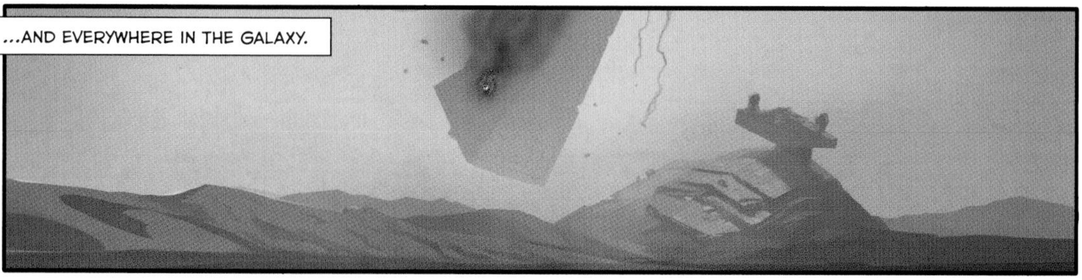
...AND EVERYWHERE IN THE GALAXY.

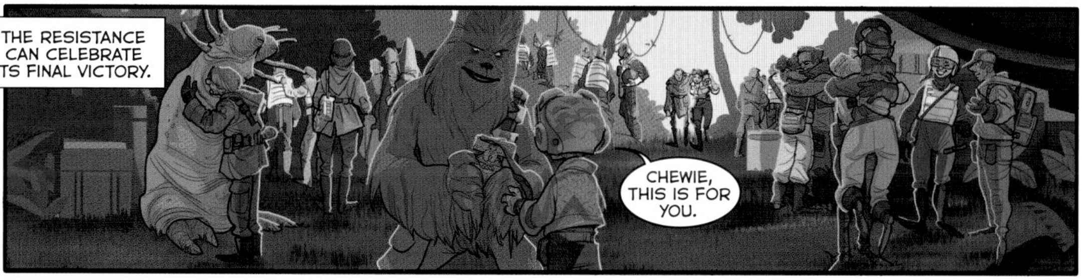
THE RESISTANCE CAN CELEBRATE ITS FINAL VICTORY.
CHEWIE, THIS IS FOR YOU.

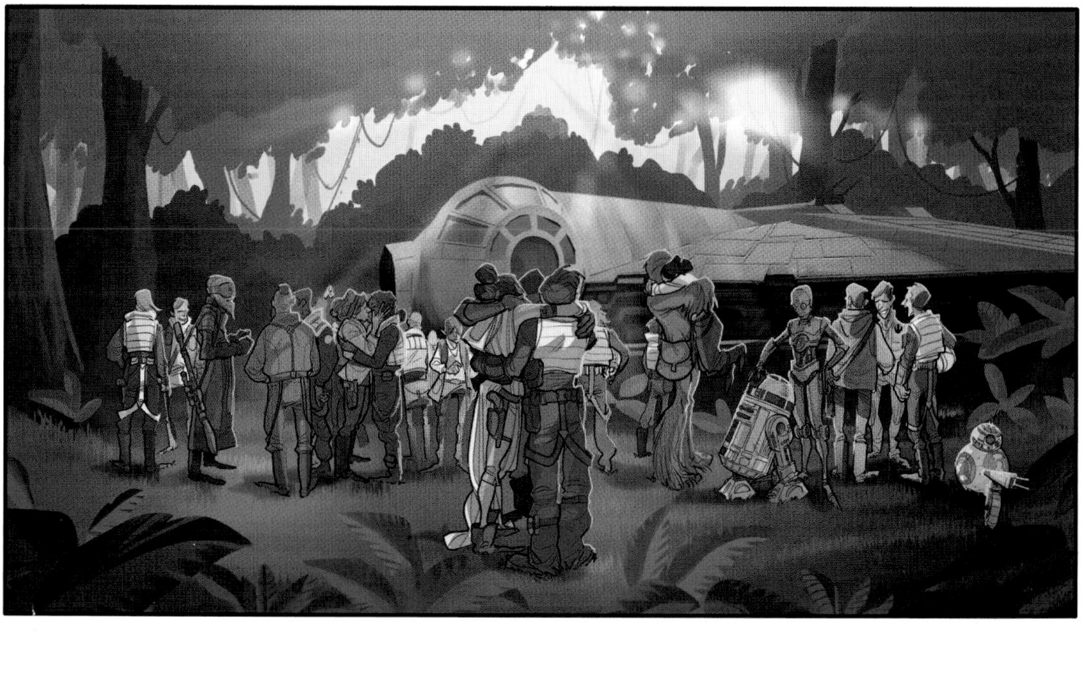

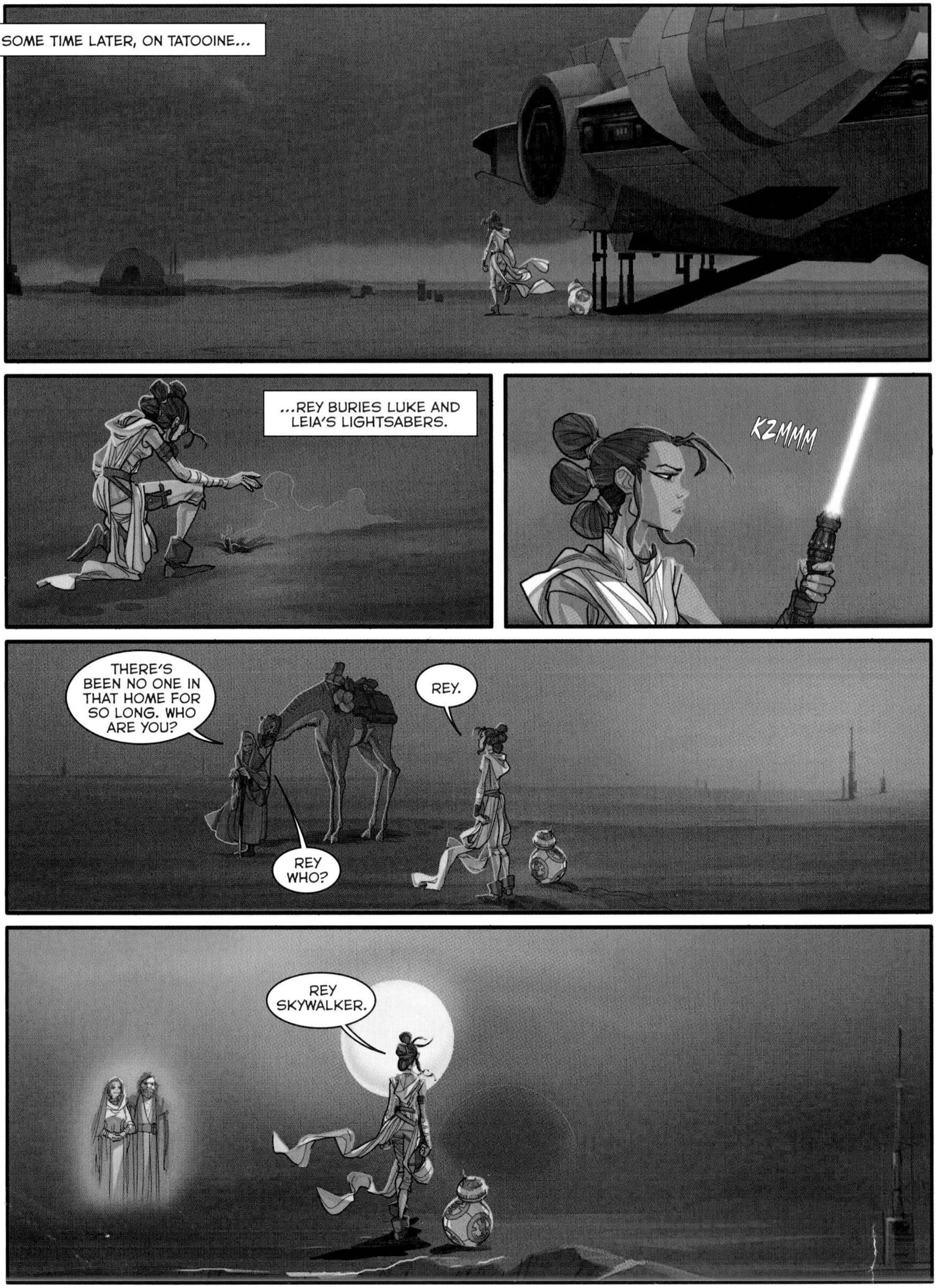
SOME TIME LATER, ON TATOOINE...
...REY BURIES LUKE AND LEIA'S LIGHTSABERS.
KZMMM
THERE'S BEEN NO ONE IN THAT HOME FOR SO LONG. WHO ARE YOU?
REY.
REY WHO?
REY SKYWALKER.

"REY, SOME THINGS ARE STRONGER THAN BLOOD. CONFRONTING FEAR IS THE DESTINY OF A JEDI."

LUKE SKYWALKER

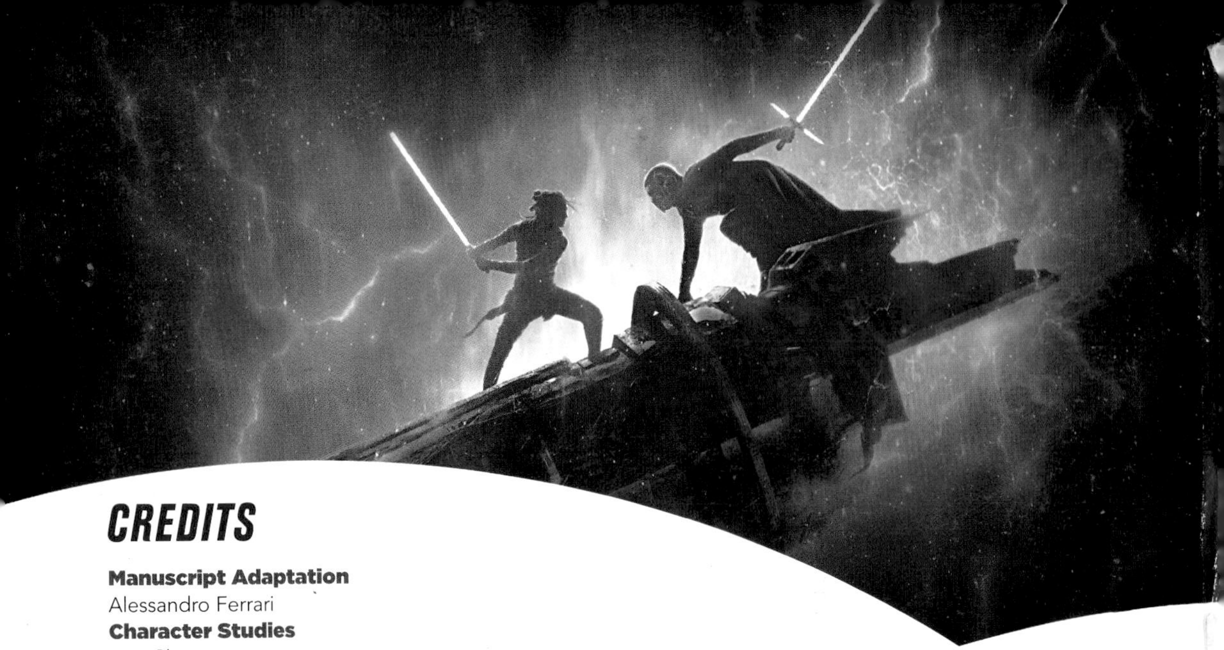

CREDITS

Manuscript Adaptation
Alessandro Ferrari

Character Studies
Igor Chimisso

Layout
Matteo Piana

Clean Up and Ink
Igor Chimisso

Paint (background and settings)
Davide Turotti

Paint (characters)
Kawaii Creative Studio

Cover
Cryssy Cheung

Special Thanks to
Michael Siglain, Robert Simpson,
James Waugh, Pablo Hidalgo,
Leland Chee, Matt Martin

Editorial Director
Bianca Coletti

Editorial Team
Guido Frazzini (Director, Comics),
Stefano Ambrosio (Executive Editor, New IP),
Carlotta Quattrocolo (Executive Editor, Franchise),
Camilla Vedove (Senior Manager, Editorial
Development),
Behnoosh Khalili (Senior Editor),
Julie Dorris (Senior Editor)
Mina Riazi (Assistant Editor)
Gabriela Capasso (Assistant Editor)

Design
Enrico Soave (*Senior Designer*)

Art
Ken Shue (VP, Global Art),
Roberto Santillo (Creative Director),
Marco Ghiglione (Creative Manager),
Manny Mederos (Senior Illustration Manager,
Comics and Magazines),
Stefano Attardi (Illustration Manager)

Portfolio Management
Olivia Ciancarelli (*Director*)

Business & Marketing
Mariantonietta Galla (Senior Manager, Franchise),
Virpi Korhonen (Editorial Manager)

For IDW:
Editors
Alonzo Simon and Zac Boone

Collection Design
Nathan Widick

Based on a story by Chris Terrio and J.J. Abrams

Based on characters created by George Lucas

For international rights, contact licensing@idwpublishing.com

ISBN: 978-1-68405-686-6

24 23 22 21   2 3 4 5

Nachie Marsham, Publisher • **Blake Kobashigawa**, VP of Sales • **Tara McCrillis**, VP Publishing Operations • **John Barber**, Editor-in-Chief • **Mark Doyle**, Editorial Director, Originals • **Erika Turner**, Executive Editor • **Scott Dunbier**, Director, Special Projects • **Mark Irwin**, Editorial Director, Consumer Products Mgr • **Joe Hughes**, Director, Talent Relations • **Anna Morrow**, Sr. Marketing Director • **Alexandra Hargett**, Book & Mass Market Sales Director • **Keith Davidsen**, Senior Manager, PR • **Topher Alford**, Sr Digital Marketing Manager • **Shauna Monteforte**, Sr. Director of Manufacturing Operations • **Jamie Miller**, Sr. Operations Manager • **Nathan Widick**, Sr. Art Director, Head of Design • **Neil Uyetake**, Sr. Art Director Design & Production • **Shawn Lee**, Art Director Design & Production • **Jack Rivera**, Art Director, Marketing

Ted Adams and Robbie Robbins, IDW Founders

www.IDWPUBLISHING.com

Facebook: facebook.com/idwpublishing • Twitter: @idwpublishing • YouTube: youtube.com/idwpublishing
Tumblr: tumblr.idwpublishing.com • Instagram: instagram.com/idwpublishing